CONGREGATIONAL LEADERSHIP 101:

A Practical Guide for
Current and Future Leaders

James L. Whitmire

http://jimwhitmire.com

jim@jimwhitmire.com

ISBN: 978-1-1-4507-5388-3

Copyright Notice

Cover design by Mike Cohenour
Interior book design by Anne Margaret Nieman

Dedication

To my "Gamaliel"
- longtime friend and fellow elder -
John Maner.

The riches of your wisdom, patience and understanding
inspired me to write this book.

Biography

I was born and raised in Ohio where my parents were members of a denominational church. While in college, I drifted away from religion altogether and into the world where I comfortably remained for ten years, until moving to Atlanta, Georgia. It was there that I met my wife, Rosalinda, who was a member of the Lord's church. Through her example, and the diligent efforts of other Christians at the Forest Park church of Christ, I was converted in 1978. That event marked the beginning of a journey that led me to the writing of this book.

After ten years of spiritual growth, I was appointed a deacon. One of my primary responsibilities was managing the production of Bible correspondence material for lost souls in the Pacific Islands. After serving as a deacon for ten years, I became an elder, and served eight years before retiring from my secular job and moving to west Georgia.

As an elder, God blessed me with the opportunity to oversee our youth and Bible School programs, Local Outreach, and Member Involvement. Part of my responsibilities included restructuring all four programs to improve their effectiveness. As a deacon and elder, I have worked with four pulpit preachers and several associate ministers. As an elder, I participated in the oversight of four missionary families working in the Pacific Islands. Over the years, God has provided amazing opportunities for me to travel overseas on eleven mission trips to various islands in the Pacific and Nicaragua and Lord willing, He will open the door for many more.

As I approached my retirement, the possibility of writing this book was on my mind. I had organized all the material I had accumulated over the years into folders and filed them neatly into plastic bins that were stacked against the wall of my home office. There they sat month after month, because I did not have enough confidence to start the process. While there seemed to be a need for a book on the practical aspects of leading a congregation of the Lord's church, the thought of me writing an entire book was just overwhelming. Articles on a single subject were one thing, but a book?

My family encouraged me to overcome my fears and begin the process. My son-in-law, Kyle, was especially helpful in suggesting that since I had written numerous articles on various subjects concerning the church; why not view each chapter as just another article. With this thought in mind, I began Chapter One and the rest is "history", as they say.

Acknowledgements

My wife, Rosalinda, provided valuable input concerning content and editing. Kyle and Brandi, my son in law and daughter, further improved the quality with their comments. Kyle devoted many hours of tireless editing that greatly enhanced the quality of this book. My youngest daughter Jessica, provided editing. My friends Sue Riley and Susan Skelton assisted me in my research. I'm thankful to my dear friend, David Riley, for his encouragement and suggestions. I can't thank Roy and Brenda Johnson enough for their encouragement and the many invaluable hours they spent assisting me with content and editing.

Preface

Over the past thirty years, I have had many experiences as a member, deacon and elder in the Lord's church that allowed me to build a substantial library of material relating to that work. Over the last year, I often stared at the boxes of material in my office and wondered if there was truly a need for a book that discussed the practical application of biblical principles that elders must take seriously as leaders of their congregations. There are a number of excellent books on church leadership like Tom Holland's Encouraging Elders and Bobby Duncan's The Elders Which Are Among You. These books provide a thorough analysis of the spiritual principles that should guide every eldership. I came to see, however, the need for a book that talked about the everyday challenges facing elders in overseeing the numerous ministries involved in a congregation. Although each congregation is autonomous, it is my hope that multiple elderships can benefit from the same source of ideas about how to organize and effectively implement various ministry activities.

It is quite possible that your congregation will not have a need for everything I have outlined for each ministry mentioned in this book or agree with the methods suggested. Hopefully it will provide useful guidance and stimulate ideas about how elderships can be more effective in carrying out their day-to-day responsibilities. I have been directly involved in or am fully aware of the success of each ministry organization discussed in this book. The structure and activities have been proven effective without a large professional staff to design and implement them.

Reading this book will take you from an overview of the current crisis in leadership within the church to the practical aspects of overseeing the everyday work of leading a congregation that is dedicated to carrying out God's mission for His church.

In addition to the information provided in the chapters, there are exhibits referenced throughout the book that the reader can review in the appendix. The exhibits include, among other things, sample letters, procedural forms, outlines, and charts that elders may wish to use for their respective congregations. Readers can modify the documents to suit local needs.

If you have questions or comments about any of the information contained in this publication please feel free to contact me at:

jwhitmire@hotmail.com

CONTENTS

CHAPTER ONE

Crisis in Leadership
Ezekiel 22:29-31

Throughout the United States there are church buildings that seat three hundred or more and are now home to fifty or fewer members of the Lord's church. My personal observations indicate this alarming trend is affecting local elderships as well. Congregations are splitting and dying throughout the brotherhood due in large part to a lack of Godly leadership. Perceptions, as previously mentioned, often influence men against stepping up and preparing themselves for this role. There is a general negative attitude toward authority today that starts in the home and has spread to our schools, society and unfortunately, the Lord's church. Then there is also the problem of priorities. Even though God and His church should always be first in our lives, (Matthew 6:33) we often fail to heed Christ's teaching on this subject (Matthew 8:19-22). Although few men would admit it, a simple lack of faith often keeps otherwise qualified men from becoming elders. Many years ago my niece gave me a plaque of Philippians 4:13 which I mounted above my home office desk. It serves as a continual reminder that our service to the Lord and His church is a "We thing, not an I thing."

Numbers 13:33 and 14:6-9 tell of the twelve spies reporting on their travel to Canaan. Only Joshua and Caleb understood that the Lord was with them. Their passion was so great that they tore their clothes as they implored their leaders to enter the Promised Land. First Samuel 17 describes the confrontation between Saul's army and the Philistines. Only David understood that Goliath's arrogance was completely without merit when he boldly asked "For who is this uncircumcised Philistine, that he should defy the armies of the living God?" (1 Samuel 17:26)

There are many negative results of this void in leadership. Qualified men will not prepare or accept the responsibility to serve. Pressure increases on those leaders currently serving, often leading to burn out and rash decisions to place unqualified individuals in leadership roles. This in turn presents golden opportunities for Satan to attack our congregations (1 Peter 5:8). All this leads to ineffective, unproductive and indecisive elders leading many of our congregations. The end result is a weakening of the Lord's church and its ability to carry out the mission that God has ordained for the body of Christ; to seek and save the lost (Luke 19:10).

Who will stand in the gap? This question was asked by God in Ezekiel 22:29-31, "The people of the land have used oppressions, committed robbery, and mistreated the poor and needy; and they wrongfully oppress the stranger. So I sought for a man among them who would make a wall, and stand in the gap before Me on behalf of the land, that I should not destroy it; but I found no one. Therefore, I have poured out My indignation on them; I have consumed them with the fire of My wrath; and I have recompensed their deeds on their own heads, says the Lord God (NKJV)." Due to the lack of one man with Godly courage, His people would spend the next seventy years in captivity.

Jeremiah faced this same challenge in Jeremiah 5:1, "Run to and fro through the streets of Jerusalem; see now and know; and seek in her open places if you can find a man, if there is anyone who executes judgment, who seeks the truth, I will pardon her (NKJV)." For the lack of one Godly leader, His wrath was brought down upon the Jewish people. Both of these Old Testament tragedies were caused by a void in leadership that was not pleasing to God.

Most of us have heard the expression, "Those who do not learn from history, are bound to repeat it. "[1] Because we have not learned from Bible history, a similar situation exists today in the Lord's church. Will we abandon our faith also? We are no longer of the same mind and heart and as a result, our influence in the world is rapidly decreasing. Christ's prayer for unity that the world might believe is becoming a faint memory. Energies are being expended dealing with strife among the saved instead of performing God's mission to seek and save the lost. Satan is overjoyed at our inability to effectively carry out our mission because of a lack of leadership in our congregations.

I would contend that virtually all problems in the church are local and the solutions to those problems are also local (Acts 14:23; Titus 1:5). Oversight of the autonomous local congregation by a plurality of qualified elders is the New Testament's one and only plan for church organization.

The challenges for today's leaders are to:

1. Work to reinstate a positive and reverent attitude toward leadership among God's people. They must set the bar high in terms of courage, integrity, commitment, and faithful service.

2. Work to create a sense of personal ownership among our members for involvement and service in the ministries of our congregations.

3. Visualize the future of their congregations. They must create and implement plans to develop future leaders. If they don't, congregations without elders will never have them and those that do will eventually be without them.

4. Identify potential leaders. Encourage and nurture them to ensure timely development of leadership qualities.

5. Continue their religious education and spiritual growth. Do not allow our potential leaders to become satisfied with status quo.

They must raise up men whose hearts are aflame with love, whose souls are full of faith and vision, whose spirits are burning with zeal, whose lives are humble and selfless. Men who know the Book, who are afraid of being ashamed and ashamed of being afraid, who are willing to come to the defense of the gospel, who will declare the whole council of God and who will count the cost and be willing to pay the price.

My challenge for tomorrow's leaders is to step up and take personal responsibility for the church and your congregation in particular. If you do not, then who will? James tells us we will be blessed IF we are doers of the Word and not hearers only (James 1:21-25). Don't underestimate what you, with God's help, can accomplish in the kingdom (Philippians 4:13).

Paul's challenge in 2 Corinthians 13:5 is to "examine yourselves as to whether you are in the faith. Test yourselves. Do you not know yourselves, that Jesus Christ is in you? Unless indeed you are disqualified (NKJV)." We have a personal responsibility to use the talents He has given us and we will be held accountable. These talents are a gift from God, what we do with these talents is our gift to God (Matthew 25:14-30).

I wonder how many of our congregations are actively preparing men to become elders, especially those without elders or with only two elders? How many, although they may not admit it, have become comfortable with the "Men's Business Meeting" style of congregational leadership? As with many activities in life, the longer we do them the harder it becomes to change those habits. The harder it becomes for two or more men to separate themselves from the crowd and take personal responsibility for leading the congregation. The harder it becomes for the congregation, especially the men, to accept and trust their leadership. Shortly after Paul established congregations on the island of Crete, he directed Titus to set in order the things that were lacking by appointing elders in every city (Titus 1:5). Who is fulfilling the role of being an example to the congregation if there are no elders (I Peter 5:3)? If a congregation is not organized as God intended or actively pursuing that organizational structure, can they avail themselves of the full spiritual blessings in Christ?

These are perilous times for the world at large and certainly the Lord's church. Both are experiencing a crisis in leadership. Personal attacks from those in opposition to current and potential political leaders discourage qualified men from serving in secular leadership positions. In much the same way, many qualified men in the church refrain from serving because of the perceived hardships associated with the work of an elder. Shortly after I was appointed an elder, news of the appointment was announced at a board meeting of a Christian organization. The general reaction from these mature Christians both surprised and disappointed me. Statements such as "buy yourself a Flak Jacket, the arrows are coming;" "say good-bye to your wife and family, you won't be seeing much of them from now on;" and "there go all your current social friends in the congregation;" were heard from around the conference table. Contrary to those comments, my eight years as an elder were, although not without challenges, the most rewarding of my Christian life. Our congregation may have been the exception, but I pray it was not. God is searching for qualified men who will stand in the gap (Jeremiah 5:1, Ezekiel 22:29-31) and lead His church.

Roman Centurions, as mentioned in the New Testament, are excellent examples of sound leadership. They spent years in preparation for this position. They led in battle from the front, wearing brightly colored plumbs on their helmets in order to inspire loyalty and ownership of the cause in those soldiers under their command. Unlike Jacob, who out of fear, allowed his wife and children to lead him toward perceived enemies, elders must be in the forefront of every battle, protecting their congregations. Although preachers are not to fulfill that role, in many congregations they perform as a de facto "pastor" because of a void in leadership. This was not God's intent.

A twenty year old single man who has completed high school and a two-year program at a preaching school may be qualified for an entry level minister's position. If that same young man desires to be an elder one day, it will require many years of spiritual growth, service, and experience that brings wisdom. It will also require the challenge of marriage and skills associated with raising a family (1 Timothy 3:1-7). We must create an environment within our congregations that encourages young men to prepare themselves for the work of an elder. As in all aspects of life, we accomplish what we plan to accomplish. That planning and the execution of that plan must originate with the elders or male leadership, including the preacher of each congregation.

As with our secular lives, balance is a key ingredient to success. Congregations that rush to appoint elders simply to have elders without adequate preparation, will often create more problems than they solve. It is much better to be scripturally unorganized, than to appoint unqualified men to serve as elders. A balanced approach to leadership includes preparing men to serve.

Elders have the awesome responsibility of protecting and feeding their congregations, as well as spreading the gospel. Their goal is to reach heaven and bring along as many souls as possible. Joshua 3:17 tells of the priests standing firm in the midst of the Jordan River so that all of Israel could cross over on dry ground to the Promised Land of Canaan. Elders have that same spiritual responsibility today. They are to lead our defense against Satan.

If we are going to be successful in developing and sustaining Godly leaders in the Lord's church we must first develop the proper attitude toward servitude. To do that, we must understand the master/servant relationship that exists between us and God. This includes not only doing His will (James 1:25), but doing it with the proper attitude (2 Corinthians 9:7).

These requirements don't just apply to our monetary giving, but are applicable to every activity in our spiritual lives, including our worship (Psalm 118:24; 122:1).Why, in a typical congregation, does attendance drop roughly thirty percent from Sunday morning to Sunday night? Why is it often difficult to motivate members to support a gospel meeting, a door knocking campaign, to teach or serve as elders or deacons? Although there are exceptions, it is apparent that, in many cases, they just enjoy doing other activities more than serving or worshipping God. While many are not willing to admit this is the reason they don't participate in certain functions, it is the unfortunate truth. There have been many seminars and workshops conducted over the years in largely futile attempts to discover the root cause of this problem and find a solution. In spite of these valiant efforts, most of the work of a congregation is still accomplished by a small minority of members.

For some time now the supposed key to church growth has been to cater to prospective members' "felt needs" by offering programs and services that satisfy the desires of today's prospects. Is this approach to church growth in accordance with Bible teaching on the purpose of the church? There is no question that Jesus taught us to be benevolent toward those less fortunate, but often the work of providing basic necessities of life somehow transforms into an attempt to fulfill everyone's wants instead of their needs.

If members of the Lord's church were asked if they desire to spend eternity in heaven, the near unanimous answer would undoubtedly be a resounding YES! If they were asked what heaven will be like, surely words such as peace, love, rest and joy would be mentioned. What will heaven really be like? Will members who do not find joy and fulfillment in serving and worshiping God on earth find joy and fulfillment in heaven? As with all spiritual questions, the answer lies in the Holy Spirit-inspired Word of God.

A search of the NKJ Bible reveals that the words "servant, serve and serving" are found 1,204 times. Granted, not all of these verses refer to serving God, but many of them do apply to our responsibilities as children of God. A similar search for the word "worship" finds its use 127 times in the Old Testament and 70 times in the New Testament. A study of applicable verses provides us insight into the relation of our efforts and attitudes on earth and our eternity in heaven. We know from Matthew 6:19-21, that Christians are to lay up spiritual treasures in heaven by living a life pleasing to God. This would obviously include prioritizing our time and efforts in serving and worshiping Him with a joyful attitude. John continues this theme in Revelation 14:13 by recalling a voice from heaven telling him those that die in the Lord will have their works follow them.

Revelation 4:10-11 captures John's vision when he sees "the four and twenty elders fall down before Him who sits on the throne and worship Him who lives forever and ever, and cast their crowns before the throne, saying: 'You are worthy, O Lord, to receive glory and honor and power;

for you created all things, and by your will they exist and were created (NKJV).'" If the twenty-four elders will be forever worshipping God, will not the remaining saved be doing this also? John continues his vision of heaven in Revelation 7:14-17, "And I said to him, Sir, you know. So he said to me, these are the ones who come out of great tribulation, and have washed their robes, and made them white in the blood of the Lamb. Therefore they are before the throne of God, and serve Him day and night in His temple: And He who sits on the throne will dwell among them. They shall neither hunger anymore nor thirst anymore; the sun shall not strike them, nor any heat; for the Lamb who is in the midst of the throne will shepherd them, and lead them to living fountains of waters. And God shall wipe away every tear from their eyes (NKJV)."

These passages confirm that those who remain faithful until death will be blessed to serve and worship God day and night forever and ever. If our number one priority here on earth is not to serve and worship God with a joyful attitude, is it not time for an honest self-examination? (2 Corinthians 13:5) Eternity is a long time.

The goals of this book are to provide congregations with guidance in applying Biblical principles to the practical aspects of developing and sustaining elders as well as assisting leaders in performing those activities involved in the daily oversight of a local congregation. I understand that you may not agree with all my recommendations and acknowledge that there are other productive ways to accomplish these functions. I do believe there is a need for this type of information if it only spurs ideas or is adapted to fit the local needs of your congregation.

The spiritual unity of a congregation results from living, worshiping and serving God in accordance with His will as found in the New Testament. Consistent integrity and courage demonstrated by the elders will result in continual trust and respect by their members. Proper application of Biblical principles to those daily activities where God allows discretion is critical to the success of each congregation's mission to seek and save the lost.

CHAPTER TWO

Developing Effective Leaders
Matthew 25:14-30

The lesson from the parable of the talents certainly applies to developing effective leaders. Christ is teaching us about accountability for developing our talents individually and, in principle, the elders' responsibility for developing effective leaders in their congregations.

In an article titled, "Something Better," Russ Burcham provides an excellent introduction to this chapter on the vital task of developing future leaders in the Lord's church.[2] He wrote of great men of faith in Hebrews who endured afflictions without receiving the Promised Messiah (Hebrews 11:39). We now have a better covenant with its abundant blessings, however along with those blessings comes a responsibility to respect the efforts of those ancient men by developing leaders better than ourselves (Hebrews 11:40).

Basics of Leadership

Commitment – "A Pledge or promise to do something." Sounds simple enough, but when it comes to serving God, it is a lifetime obligation that must be taken seriously. Peter instructs newborn Christians to desire the sincere milk of the Word in order to grow spiritually (1 Peter 2:2). This is a continuous process that should lead each man to ever higher levels of spiritual maturity throughout his life if he is committed to faithfully serving God on a daily basis. It is imperative that we instill and continually reinforce in our young men the importance of commitment. The world's carnal enticements are pulling many of our children away from the church. We must teach them that a Christian cannot serve two masters by keeping one foot in the world and the other in the church (Matthew 6:24 & Luke 14:30). They must have their priorities right before they leave home. This task is the primary responsibility of the parents, but the church also has a role in nurturing their spiritual growth.

This commitment involves a love for God's Word that includes obedience to His commands (John 14:15). He expects us to grow spiritually in order to reach the potential that God has instilled in each of us (Hebrews 5:12, 13). Each man must perform a continual self-examination (Galatians 6:4). He should consider the following questions: "What is my vision for our congregation over the next one to ten years (Galatians 6:4)?" "What part will I play in reaching our goals?" Am I satisfied with my level of service?" "Am I satisfied with my rate of spiritual growth?" "Do I truly believe Philippians 4:13?" People often lose eye contact with you when they are asked a question they don't want to truthfully answer. Can you pass the "look in the mirror" test when asking yourself the above questions?

Involvement – Commitment leads to involvement when Christians overcome inactivity (Christians at rest tend to stay at rest) and become more productive in meaningful ministries. The excuse for lack of involvement by many members is that the church is a "volunteer organization" and it is a foregone conclusion that eighty percent of the work will be done by twenty percent of the members. The Bible does not support that contention. In contrast to the 1204 references to service, the word volunteer is found once and it does not relate to congregational membership. God created man with free will, but do we as faithful Christians have the option not be involved in the work of the church? As always, Christ provides the perfect example of a life of service to God (Mark 10:42,45, John 13:12-17). James 1:22-25 tells us that spiritual blessings flow to those who are doers of the Word and not hearers only.

Growth – Commitment will lead to involvement and involvement will naturally lead to spiritual growth. In Luke 2:46-49, we read of young Jesus spending three days in the temple listening and asking questions of religious leaders. This desire for knowledge led to an increase in wisdom, stature, and favor with God and men. We see in Philippians 3:12-14, that the Apostle Paul was committed to spiritual growth as a lifelong pursuit. Peter exhorts us in 1 Peter 2:1-5 to lay aside evil thoughts and actions to seek maturity through continual study of God's Word. He compares this to building a house with Christ as the foundation (1 Peter 2:4, 5; Matthew 21:42).

There are numerous tools available to aid us in our spiritual growth. They all have one drawback; they must be used to provide any benefit. It all starts with Bible study on a continual basis. If we just read the Book without taking the time to meditate upon it, we barely scratch the surface of the mind of God (Philippians 4:8). One of the pleasures I've found in retirement is the extra time to study God's Word and to meditate on the richness of His inspirational teachings. Books, magazines, websites, lectureships, seminars, and other edifying resources will expand on Bible teaching. Daily prayer will bring us closer to God as we deal with the constant struggles of living in the world but not becoming part of the world. Social fellowship with other Christians will influence and edify us. Consider short-term mission trips locally or overseas. I always come back spiritually refreshed and uplifted after a mission trip.

Desire – Commitment leads to involvement, which leads to growth, which should lead to a desire to be all we can be for the Lord. For those men with the talent and opportunity, this desire should also include leadership. Professional trips and travels have given me the opportunity to visit many congregations throughout the United States. Although each group is unique in its own way, at least one common thread runs through most of them – a lack of qualified leaders. More often than not, the one lacking qualification is that of desire. I often heard this frustrated comment from current elders, "We have qualified men but they just do not have the desire to be elders." Is this a valid reason or an excuse? Will the Lord accept this response on Judgment Day?

When I asked these leaders why otherwise qualified men do not desire the office of elder, their responses were remarkably similar: "I don't want the stress." "I'm not willing to give up that much of my personal time." "I don't want to be responsible for other people's souls." "I don't want to lose my friends." As you probably noticed, these responses are self-centered not Christ-centered.

Meeting the qualifications to become an elder is directly related to spiritual growth. Since the power to impart spiritual gifts ended long ago, no one today is qualified to be an elder immediately after baptism (1 Corinthians 13:8-11; 1 Timothy 3:6). Men must grow into the job. The Bible is filled with teaching about our individual responsibilities to grow spiritually throughout our physical lives (Ephesians 4:11-16; Hebrews 5:12-14; 1Peter 2:2). Paul strove for spiritual perfection his entire life

(Philippians 3:13, 14). Why would this teaching apply to other areas and not to our desire to serve God at the highest possible level?

Do we not understand the application of the parable of the talents as it applies to the qualifications for elders? Most men understand their responsibilities as related to other qualifications, such as becoming temperate, sober minded, hospitable and able to teach, but they often overlook the bedrock qualification – developing a desire to serve.

The generic definition of desire is to "crave or long for." Vines Expository Dictionary tells us in the case of 1 Timothy 3:1, that the meaning here is significantly different. It is to "desire earnestly" as Paul desired to be with Christ (Philippians 1:23). It stresses the inward impulse rather than the object being desired.

James A. Garfield, our 20th president, and a former elder in the church, was believed to have said that he was stepping down from the highest office on earth to accept the position of President of the United States. How could participation in the oversight of a small group of Christians be more important than being Commander-in-Chief of the most powerful nation in the world? Few people outside the church understand the gravity of that remark, and unfortunately, many men in the church fail to comprehend it. The work of an elder was so highly esteemed, even in the first century, that it had already grown into a saying: "If a man desires the position of a bishop, he desires a good work."

Are not the problems of the church and solutions to those problems local? Is there any other organizational structure authorized by God? Qualified leadership in our congregations is critical to the spiritual health of the Lord's body. Men who meet the other qualifications should strive to develop a desire to serve as elders. I would ask those men to search their hearts for the reasons they lack this desire. Is it a convenient cop out to hide selfish motives for maintaining their current life style?

Developing desire is within man's control. To cultivate a desire to lead one must:

1. *See the need* – Once Paul established churches on the island of Crete, he instructed Titus to set in order the things that were lacking by appointing elders in every city (Titus 1:5). We no longer have miraculous gifts to prepare men to be elders, but God, through the Holy Spirit has provided us with the tools to develop leaders for our congregations. It is His pattern for the church that each

local congregation be overseen by qualified elders and we have a responsibility to prepare ourselves and others to accomplish this critical work.

2. *See it as a work not a position* – During my career, I worked with someone who struggled under a tyrannical manager for several years before his manager retired. When my colleague was promoted to the manager position his attitude was that he had "arrived" and was now going to sit back and enjoy the fruits of his labors and that is what he did for much of his career. This is not what the Lord has in mind for those ordained as elders in His church (1Timothy 3:1). We must see this as an opportunity to lead the congregation in service to God in every way. We must continue to grow spiritually so that an honest annual self-evaluation will confirm that we are better elders this year than we were last year. In order to accomplish this goal, we must plan each year's activities with continual growth in mind.

3. *See the importance of church* – In this fast paced world, it is easy to take important relationships for granted. Many marriages have soured and failed because one or both parties did not continually give it the attention it deserved and required. We, the church, are the bride of Christ and this relationship should be our number one priority (Matthew 6:33 & Ephesians 5:22-27). We must truly understand the critical nature of the Lord's church as it relates to our eternal destiny (Isaiah 2:2).

4. *See the eternal consequences* – A study of the shepherd/sheep relationship in the first century helps us to fully understand the importance of developing qualified elders. Wolves are always looking for opportunities to attack the flock from within or without (Acts 20:28-31). Paul warned the elders at Ephesus for three years about this danger. The Hebrew writer reminds Christians that elders will give an account for the souls of their flock on Judgment Day (Hebrews 13:17). The goal of shepherds should be to get to heaven and take as many of their flock with them as possible.

5. *See the privilege of leading God's people* – Instead of listening to those negative comments about the pitfalls of leading the church, focus on the honor and privilege of overseeing a local congregation of this holy nation of priests (1 Peter 2:9).

6. *See the obligation* – God is not frivolous. He gave us talents and the ability to develop them for a reason (Matthew 25:14-30). He expects each of us, as the Army commercial said, to "be all you can be" in His army. If we are nurturing the proper attitude toward service to God, we will look forward with joy to developing our talents in order to serve at the highest level possible during our time on this earth. Our just God will hold us accountable for how we utilize our talents in the church, for which He paid such an unbelievable price.

7. *See the rewards of serving* – If we willingly and eagerly prepare and serve as examples to the flock, there will be rewards both on earth and in heaven (1 Peter 5:1-4). The fellowship and bond of serving in a unified eldership is something that I will treasure the rest of my life. There is the satisfaction of being good stewards of the Lord's resources (time, energy, people, money, etc.) that maximize the productivity of a congregation in doing the Lord's work. Matthew Henry, in his commentary on Timothy, said it well: "If a man desire [the work of an elder], he should earnestly desire it for the prospect he has of bringing greater glory to God, and of doing the greatest good to the souls of men by this means.³" The crown mentioned by Peter is one given to heroes or conquerors NOT royalty. It is a perpetual and immortal reward for faithful and valued service.

Plan for Leadership Development

The best way to get from where you are now to where you want to be is to develop and follow a reliable guide whether that is a map or GPS for traveling or a plan to develop leaders in the Lord's church. As Christians, we all have an individual responsibility to grow spiritually (Hebrews 5:12, 13 & 1 Peter 2:2). Elders should also be involved in the spiritual development of potential leaders in their congregation by doing the following:

1. Work to create and maintain an atmosphere of trust and respect for the eldership by continually exhibiting courage and integrity. Young men will aspire to a work that they see as admirable and rewarding.

2. Implement a plan to identify and develop future leaders. Start by making a matrix of potential leaders' names, time frames, strengths/weaknesses, and elder/mentors (Exhibit 1). Time frames for meeting the qualifications for an elder can be short-term (1-3 years); medium-term (3-5 years); and long-term (5-10 years). These

time frames should be determined by a consensus of the elders for each man being considered. Individual elders would be assigned to mentor each man along his developmental path. Developmental assignments for each man would then be implemented. The progress of each man should be reviewed annually and the matrix updated.

3. Meet with short-term prospects and their wives to develop a personalized plan that would include timetables (teach an adult class within one year), milestones (complete reading of assigned books), developmental assignments (work in benevolence, Bible school, local outreach, etc.), and a frank discussion of their strengths and weaknesses. Periodic future meetings (every six months) would be held to review progress and make necessary adjustments.

4. Develop broader and more flexible plans for medium-term and long-term prospects. Areas such as study habits (daily Bible reading), rotational assignments, books, lectureships, forums, and short-term mission trips should be considered. Keep in mind that leadership development is an extended process. God spent eighty years preparing Moses for forty years of service. Also, remember that leadership character can be developed. Don't dismiss a young man's potential simply because of how he acts and thinks today. Stress to these young men the necessity of being socially involved with members of all ages, educational and career backgrounds and recreational interests. It is human nature to gravitate toward those people or families with whom we share common backgrounds and interests, but an elder must be known and trusted by all his congregation and to accomplish that he must continually be among all of them.

5. Periodically conduct formal classes for prospective elders and deacons. *Personal invitations* should be extended to potential leaders to attend these classes with the understanding that there is no commitment by either party on future positions. An open invitation to the men of the congregation is optional.

John Gardner, writing in reference to corporate and government executives, says, "One reason corporate and governmental bureaucracies stagnate is the assumption by line executives that, given their rank and authority, they can lead without being leaders. They cannot. They can be given subordinates, but they cannot be given a following; a following must be earned. Surprisingly, many of them do not even know they are not leading. They mistake the exercise of authority for leadership, and as long as they persist in that mistake they will never learn the art of turning subordinates into followers.[4]"

This same situation can occur in the church when elders believe their appointment automatically makes them leaders with a faithful following. "Leaders without followers is an oxymoron but a situation that is all too frequently encountered in the church. The true leader is the person whose voice the sheep hear and follow.[5]"

Future leaders must step up and take personal responsibility for the development of their talents. Start now to prepare yourselves for leadership. You will not wake up one day and suddenly be prepared to lead. Accidental leaders are rarely effective leaders. Formulate a development plan and work that plan. James clearly states the requirements for receiving God's blessings: we must hear and *do* (James 1:22-25). Action is required. Nehemiah prayed to God for protection from his enemies while the people rebuilt the walls around Jerusalem, but he also posted guards. If we do our part, God will do His part. Almost every potential elder has doubts about his ability to lead a congregation. Keep in mind there are other elders to share the responsibility and God is with you (Philippians 4:13). Honestly examine yourself with the help of your family.

CHAPTER THREE

Sustaining Effective Leaders
1 Timothy 5:17

Paul is teaching us that consistent integrity and courage by elders will result in continual trust and respect for them by their congregation.

I believe the over-arching principle for sustaining effective leadership in a congregation is balance. If you have ever been a parent, teacher or baby-sitter, you have probably used the phrase "color between the lines." If you work or have worked for corporate America, you probably have heard or used the now outmoded phrase "think outside the box." Buzz words and phrases come and go periodically in an effort to keep us all motivated. Having been a parent and now grandparent as well as spending much of my professional career dealing with those inside the Washington Beltway, I have heard both phrases often. As leaders, there are times when we need to color between the lines and times when we need to think outside the box. The key to success in any venture is to know which of these applies in any given situation.

While pondering the current state of the Lord's church, I began to see a correlation between these two phrases. Are we the same strong, vibrant, growing church that we have been in years past? Most would agree we are not, which should cause all of us to reflect on the possible causes of our current dilemma.

I have read many fine articles that went into great detail analyzing this problem. These writings remind me of some of the management articles I have read over the years with deep thought, numerous details and weighty conclusions. All these business publications aside, the two that helped the most in my secular career were the "One Minute Manager" and "Management Time: Who's got the Monkey?" These were short, simple, straightforward publications full of common sense. Applying these same principles to the church, we may discover that our problems and potential solutions are not as complicated as some would have us to believe.

It seems today that many of our congregations spend much of their time worrying about members of the church "coloring between the lines"(legalists) while others spend most of their time "thinking outside the box" (progressives/change agents). As with most activities in life, when we get out of balance, we usually fail to achieve success. If we are to be the church God would have us to be, we must search His Word because we know that it contains the answers to our problems (Acts 17:11 & 2 Peter 1:3). If regaining our balance is the solution to our current problems, then we must emulate the perfectly balanced Word of God. Examples throughout the Bible show God's people coloring between the lines and thinking outside the box at appropriate times and with appropriate subjects.

Moses directed Israel not to change God's commands (Deuteronomy 4:2). They were to teach these commands to their children lest they raise up a generation that did not know God (Deuteronomy 4:10 & Judges 2:10). Paul warned the elders at Ephesus and the Galatians to watch for those who would rise up from within and without to pervert God's Word (Acts 20:28-31 & Galatians 1:6-10). John warned us at the end of Revelation not to change what had been written by the inspired writers (Revelation 22:18,19). In other words, color between the lines.

Everywhere the apostles went, they adapted their style and method of teaching and preaching to the culture at hand. They obviously had great success in reaching every person in the world with their message (Colossians 1:23). In writing to the Jews, Matthew often quoted from the Old Testament in his efforts to convince his readers that Jesus was the Messiah predicted by the prophets. He adapted the style and format of his message to his audience. Mark and Luke made few references to the Old Testament because they were writing primarily to the Gentiles who had little knowledge or interest in it. In teaching the Greeks in Athens, Paul used their unknown god to teach about the One true God.

In other words, these men were thinking outside the box, being creative in determining the best way to reach various groups with the same message. Who could have dreamed years ago that our congregations and missionaries would be reaching the lost throughout the world by television, radio, and the internet?

The key to our success in glorifying God may well lie in the simple principle of balance. I would ask those who continually police the brotherhood how much of their time and effort is spent reaching and teaching the lost? I would also ask those who spend their time spreading the "unity in diversity" doctrine of fellowshipping with denominations, when was the last time they considered the admonitions of Moses, Paul and John not to tamper with God's Word? Is it ever wise to see how close we can get to the edge of righteousness?

Let us seek the old paths in doctrine while seeking new paths in discretionary areas to improve the oversight of our congregations in the mission that God has set out for the church (Luke 19:10).

With those thoughts in mind, we will now discuss the specifics of sustaining effective leaders.

Secular vs. Spiritual Leadership

A. Overlapping circles of responsibilities/qualifications

1. *Vision* – Effective leaders in any endeavor must periodically step back from the day to day oversight of their operations and look beyond the horizon at what they want to see their congregation become in three, five, or ten years. Do they dream of a new building, oversight of missionaries, starting a Christian school, or campus ministry? Turning those visions into reality requires a plan with milestones to gauge the progress of that plan during development. Plan your work then work your plan, it is as simple as that. The format for planning retreats will be discussed later.

2. *Organization* – The Lord expects us to be good stewards of our time and energy as well as our finances. Sound organization of each ministry will result in the maximum productivity from those efforts. Being efficient is not enough; we must be effective in accomplishing God's work of edifying, evangelizing and benevolence. We will go into detail about how to apply Bible principles to various ministries n later chapters.

3. *Experience* – There is no hard fast rule about when a man has enough experience to be an effective leader. In our fast paced business world, we see "child prodigies". That does not necessarily make them strong leaders. As discussed earlier, it is vitally important for

potential leaders in a congregation to work in various ministries while preparing for leadership. Leaders must also be grounded in God's Word and that takes time and effort. Wisdom is the application of knowledge and knowledge takes time to acquire. I served with elders that had decades of experience and that wealth of knowledge had been invaluable in dealing with the many challenges we faced on a continual basis.

4. *Analytical Skills* – Even small to medium size congregation's deal with hundreds of thousands of dollars in contributions and numerous local and distant ministries that are funded by those contributions. Many members and missionaries of the church, who have diverse personalities and cultural backgrounds, work in those ministries. Effective leaders must have the capability to oversee these efforts. That includes funding them and ensuring the people involved are properly trained and continually motivated. Elders must be able to understand the nature of interpersonal relationships, break down problems to their lowest level, and clearly determine solutions.

B. Different responsibilities/qualifications

1. *Board of Directors vs. Eldership* – Years ago the congregation we attended hired an associate minister and I asked him how often he met with his previous elders. He answered, "Whenever I could find them." Apparently his elders did not meet on a regular basis and had relatively little involvement in the day to day activities of their congregation. I have served on the Board of Directors for two church related organizations. We met about every 3-4 months to discuss policy, finances, personnel and programs but left the day to day operation of the agencies to the Executive Director and his staff. This is not the type of oversight that the Lord had in mind for elders in His church. Metaphorical references to shepherds and sheep in describing the elders' relationship to their congregations underscores this point. Shepherds lead by developing a trusting relationship with their flock, and they do this by spending much time among them. This same technique should be applied to elders and their flock if they want to establish a trusting relationship. We will discuss in detail how to accomplish this in later chapters.

2. *Office vs. "Work"* – It is interesting to note that Vine indicates on page 443 of Vine's Expository Dictionary of Biblical Words that there is no word in the original Greek for "office" in 1 Timothy 3:1.

The Revised Version rightly omits the word "office" and translates the verb diaknoeo, "to serve" in verses 10 and 13. The Lord intended for elders to be "verbs" not "nouns." It is not an honorary position or office, but a "good work." As programs and people are put into place the work of an elder evolves into one of guidance, mentoring, oversight and envisioning, but should never become detached from the daily functioning of a congregation.

3. *Source of Power* – Personality/Relationships vs. Scriptures. Secular leaders often derive much of their power from their personalities and relationships with others inside and outside of their organizations. This power is sometimes abused due to greed and lust. The Holy Spirit warns elders in 1 Peter 5:3 not to "lord over the flock" but be examples to them. Thankfully the Bible provides leaders with distinct lines of authority when it comes to areas of discretion and non-discretion. Elders must hold fast to sound doctrine, but allow themselves to be creative in areas of discretion (2 Timothy 1:13).

4. *Personal Relationships* – Distant vs. Familiar. Secular Boards of Directors generally do not have much contact with the staff members of their organization. That is not their function. In the church, it is critical that elders establish and continually work to maintain personal relationships with members of their flock (John 10:5; 13:34, 35). There is only one way for a shepherd to smell like his sheep and that is to spend as much time as possible among them. This task becomes more difficult as the congregation grows in number and requires adjustments in the elders' methods for maintaining personal relationships with their members. We will discuss ways to do this in later chapters.

5. *Leadership Methods*

   a. Drive vs. Lead (force/order vs. motivate/encourage) - It is interesting that secular leaders are sometimes referred to as "cowboys", but rarely are they described as "shepherds." They often lead by intimidation, competition and peer pressure. An important point to keep in mind is that cowboys "drive" cattle from the rear while shepherds "lead" sheep from the front. Sheep follow their leader because they know and trust him while cattle are driven through fear and coercion.

   b. General vs. Specific Experience – Living in the Atlanta area, I have always taken an interest in Delta Air Lines. Some years ago they hired a CEO with no previous airline experience. His previous experience was in Public Utilities and Finance. It is not unusual for large companies to hire executives with little operational experience in that company's business. A general management background seems to qualify people for these type positions. He did not stay with Delta long before taking a position with another company. It seems like business executives are similar to professional baseball managers in that they are often hired to be fired. The opposite approach should be taken when appointing elders. They should be very familiar with the members of the congregation, its' various ministries, and personnel. I have heard it said by one elder, that his eldership would not appoint a man unless he had "grown up" in that congregation. While selecting someone who recently placed membership at a church is unwise, there is no scriptural requirement for his restriction. When you are selecting potential elders consideration must be given to experience, availability, need, and biblical qualifications.

    c. Coercion vs. motivation – Secular leaders is often driven by different motives than spiritual leaders. Money, power, influence, prestige and pride are driving forces behind the desire for promotion and advancement to positions of higher authority. The motives for a man desiring the work of an elder must be selfless service; a man after God's own heart. He must be committed to using all his God-given talents to glorify the King.

6. *Servant Heart vs. Master Attitude* – An elder must have a serving heart (Mark 10:45). He must be humble and courageous at the same time. He must be made of velvet and steel and have the wisdom to know when each is needed.

The Challenge of Effective Leadership

A. Reaching consensus in decision making

1. *Perils of leadership by committee* – It has been said of the Italian dictator, Mussolini, that he was cruel and oppressive but at least the trains ran on time. One man rule, in the short run, can be efficient, but it is rarely effective in the long run in carrying out the will of the people or certainly the Will of God (Acts 14:23 & Philippians 2:2-4). That being said, there are challenges to effective leadership

by committee. Just because the Lord directed the oversight of local congregations by a plurality of elders, does not mean success will come easily. Elderships must often deal with competing priorities of individual elders. One elder's favorite ministry might be foreign missions while another's is the Bible school program. Selfishness, "office politics", internal alliances and even manipulations within an eldership can lead to tension and the inability to accomplish the work of the church. Committees are often slow to react to situations when consensus cannot be reached on an appropriate course of action. I witnessed this many times in my career with the federal government as representatives from the various Military Service Branches vied for their competing priorities. Sometimes one elder might think he is the "de facto" chief elder and expect to get his way in any disagreement. The productivity of an eldership can suffer when one or more men adhere to the "pie" philosophy of leadership, wherein their "slice of the pie" becomes smaller if someone else's idea or plan is accepted. All individual elders are part of the eldership, and one elder does not lose respect or influence when another elder's idea or suggestion is adopted instead of his own.

2. *How to make it work in the eldership* - John Wooden, the most successful college basketball coach in history, describes the importance of leadership in Wooden on Leadership. "The best leaders," he writes, "are more interested in finding what's right than in always being right. They understand how much more can be accomplished if no one cares who gets credit.[6]" Effective congregational leadership starts with each man humbling himself before the eldership to which he is subject as a member of the congregation, just as all Christians should humble themselves before Christ (James 4:10). Love and respect must be shown for your fellow elders (John 13:34,35). Everyone should be unified in their priorities for the congregation (Luke 19:10). It is then the task of leadership to determine the best methods, use of resources and application of Biblical principles to accomplish those goals established by the elders. The best course of action for any venture at the congregational level and indirectly the universal church, is a win for all regardless of who devised the idea or who may get the credit. Although the word synergy is often over used in business and management discussions, elders should understand the impact it can have on the success of congregational leadership. The wisdom

35

of collective decisions far surpasses the abilities of individual elders. We should never underestimate the power of the Lord working through Godly men (Philippians 4:13). There will be times when complete consensus is not attainable and a formal vote is necessary. There is nothing inherently wrong with voting as long as all the elders support the final approved decision and stand behind that decision even if questioned by members of the congregation.

B. Implementing Decisions/Delegating Responsibility & Authority

1. *Develop and maintain the trust and respect of the congregation* – This obviously does not require perfection, but it does require a high level of integrity and courage by the elders. Who you are as a husband, father, provider, and member will affect your relationship with the congregation. There are detrimental effects when an eldership loses the trust of the congregation. Minor issues become major points of contention when members don't fully believe they can trust the elders to lead their souls to heaven. Sheep only follow shepherds they know and trust. It is critical that elders make consistent application of Biblical principles in dealing with the day-to-day oversight of their congregation. Also they must show "one face to the congregation". Private decision making rarely starts with complete consensus, but once a decision is made it is the "elders' decision" and all must enthusiastically support it before the congregation. Don't succumb to certain members with personal agendas that may try to influence your support of the elders' position.

2. *Create a "sense of ownership" for the works of the various ministries of your congregation* – Start by including those most responsible for implementing these activities as early as possible in the development process. Ask for their input and carefully consider their ideas. Provide them the authority to successfully carry out their assigned responsibilities. Fully explain the reasons for new ministries to the congregation and how they will support the work of the church. Some years ago our local outreach team decided to propose a billboard designed by our members that would rotate to a different location around our area every three months for a year. We promoted it to the congregation during development and the initial placement. The first time it was moved one of our deacons asked, "What happened to our billboard?" I knew that he had "taken ownership" of that outreach effort by subconsciously using "our" not "your" or "the congregation's" when he referred to the billboard.

Input plus responsibility plus authority equals ownership. When members input is solicited and they are given responsibility and authority to implement ministry actions, they will take ownership of the goals established for that ministry.

3. *The rifle approach vs. the shotgun approach* - As many of you know, a rifle fires one bullet at a single target, and a shotgun fires many pellets over a wide area. These two weapons have distinctly different functions. Use a "rifle" approach instead of a "shotgun" approach when recruiting members to serve in various capacities within your ministries. How many times have you heard an elder or deacon stand in the pulpit and use the "shotgun" approach by asking for people to sign up for various works in the church? Most people are thinking he is talking to the person seated next to them. Everybody's business is nobody's business. I have found the "rifle" approach to be much more effective. Decide who you would like to be involved in various programs and in what capacity then consider their possible responses to your initial request. Be prepared to thoughtfully encourage them to participate. Then ask to meet with them privately, explain the need and why they are the best possible choice for the position in question. I experienced a very high success rate with this approach.

4. *Take direct responsibility for solving the "80/20" problem that exists within congregations* – In most churches, eighty percent of the work is done by twenty percent of the members. As we all know, this often leads to burnout, ineffectiveness and a lack of cohesion within the congregation. Start by asking yourself, "What am I doing or not doing as a leader that prevents members from assuming responsibility and reaching new levels of involvement?" "Am I matching talents with ministries?" "Am I providing enough authority with the responsibility I am assigning?" "Am I micromanaging a ministry?" "Am I allowing my ego or insecurities to affect my involvement plans for other members?"

5. *"Am I relying on the "shotgun" approach previously mentioned?"* Understand that members are connected to the congregation's successes and failures when they are held personally accountable. They will see themselves as instruments of their own destiny. In other words, they know that the success of their ministry is directly dependent on them.

6. *Leaders must understand their tasks*

    a. Determine direction. Strike a balance between micro managing every detail and an aloof "Board of Directors" style of oversight. Delegate the daily operation of your ministries to deacons and other qualified people within your congregation, and concentrate on maintaining a vision for the congregation and planning how to accomplish those goals.

    b. Continually look for ways to remove obstacles (financial, personnel, coordination, and access) that prevent members from focusing their efforts on meeting the milestones established by the elders for the work of each ministry. Ask them about their responsibilities; observe meetings, Bible classes, etc. to gauge progress firsthand and make suggestions where appropriate. Subtle periodic inquires about their progress can be a great motivator to stay on track with the assignment.

    c. Place the responsibility for implementing and sustaining programs with the ministry leaders and empowering with the elders. Beware of upward delegation that can rob elders of their limited hours available for overseeing the congregation.[7]

    d. Continue to coach and support after providing direction, removing obstacles and empowering ministry leaders. As mentioned in the One Minute Manager, leaders should "try to catch [members] doing something right" in order to encourage their involvement.[8]

Maturing Congregational Leaders

I had the privilege to know a wonderful man who spent 85 of his 96 years as a Christian and 30 of those years as an elder. He was legally blind for the last years of his life. He was a good friend and I always enjoyed talking with him at services each week. He would tell me what books of the Bible he was studying by listening to audio tapes and exclaim how much more he had to learn about God! I miss his example but he continues to inspire me every day to grow spiritually.

Elders must understand that they have not "arrived" the day they are appointed to this ever challenging work. We all must continue our spiritual growth as long as we are capable of learning (Philippians 3:12-

14). In addition to daily Bible reading make time for reading pertinent books and periodicals (see suggestions in Exhibit 2) as well as attending at least one good lectureship and area workshop each year. Much of a leader's spiritual growth is attained informally on a day-to-day basis and can be compared to the growth of a tree (Psalm 1:1-3). We must first grow down to establish our root system and build a solid foundation upon which to grow (Titus 2:11,12). This requires continual self-examination to develop motivation and self-discipline. Now we can concentrate on growing up toward God and out toward others (Matthew 22:37-39). We grow closer to God through prayer, meditation and Bible study and closer to others by spending time visiting, attending church related social events and being among the first to arrive for services and the last to leave. Also make yourself available for impromptu meetings as members have need.

Successful elders practice the four M's of leadership:

1. Mentor – Make yourself available formally and informally to teach, encourage, and counsel members. Meet people for lunch during the week or invite them to your home. This gives you time to really get to know them and move your relationship beyond the "Hello, how are you?" stage established at worship and Bible study times.

2. Motivate – Leaders continually have opportunities to inspire members with both the "shotgun" and "rifle" methods discussed earlier. Show a positive "can do" spirit that will infect others. Always remember that leaders set the bar for commitment and involvement.

3. Mingle – As I have mentioned, spend as much time among the congregation as possible. At least one elder should attend every church related social function, as well as ministry meetings. This is especially important to those that are under your direct oversight to demonstrate your active interest in these works. Elders should disperse themselves among the members at social functions in order to develop closer personal relationships with them. Visit members on a regular basis and have them into your home.

4. Model – Can you say to your members "Imitate me as I imitate Christ?" (1Corinthians 11:1). Strive to serve as a continual example to others by your integrity, service to God and commitment to living a Christian life of morality.

Traits of Effective Elders

1. Develop the "lost art" of being a good listener – Convey body language that sends the speaker a message that you care about what they have to say; that their message is important to you; that you are concerned about their welfare. Don't give the impression you are simply waiting for an opportunity to break in and start talking or that you are only thinking about how you will respond.

2. Develop a "thick skin" – Learn not to wear your feelings on your shirt sleeves. Don't be quickly offended by criticism, constructive or otherwise. Don't get immediately defensive when coming under verbal attack. Often people will settle down after an initial outburst and discuss their problems rationally if the atmosphere is calm and non-threatening.

3. Learn to be dispassionate – Becoming emotionally involved in every issue that comes before the eldership is a quick ticket to burnout. Different people and issues affect elders in different ways. Let another elder take the lead if you are unable to separate your emotions from the problem-solving process.

4. Be "people-friendly" – Elders' primary responsibility is to shepherd their flock and to do that they must "live among the sheep" and get to know them well. An aloof, "hard to approach" elder will lose much of his effectiveness in this area of work.

5. Understand that elders are always teaching when they are in public regardless of the situation – Elders hold positions of substantial influence whether they are formally teaching a class or personal Bible study or simply going about their daily routine. They are held to a higher standard because of their ability to influence others.

6. Continually check to make sure your priorities are in the proper order – The church should come first in your lives (Matthew 6:33). A good way to view Sunday is that it is the Lord's Day and plan on giving most all of your time that day to the Lord's work. Strive to maintain balance in your efforts to lead the congregation. It is easy to gravitate toward those ministries that you enjoy. Working with less popular ministries may not be as exciting or positive as evangelism, but they are just as important and deserve our best efforts.

7. Be slow to speak and quick to listen – Words spoken in haste or anger can never be retracted after the damage is done. A measured response is almost always the best reply (James 3:3-8).

8. Be a daily Bible reader – It is easy to get caught up in the everyday activities of leadership and forget to take the private time to meditate on God's Word in order to extract deeper meaning from the scriptures.

9. Pray daily – Never underestimate the power of prayer. Understand that serving as an elder is a "we" thing not an "I" thing. God and your fellow elders will "hold up your arms" as you fight the good fight (Hebrews 13:5).

10. Develop a reputation as a trustworthy person – This may be the most important quality of a leader in the Lord's church. Members will only follow elders they trust to watch for their souls. Be men of integrity so that your word is always creditable. This kind of reputation is not easily attained, but easily lost and almost impossible to regain.

11. Learn how to be an effective motivator – Elders don't have financial or legal power over other members. Most members will only be as committed as their elders or less. Elders must inspire them to action by their example.

12. Develop the ability to plan and execute – Lead by the five P's, "Proper preparation prevents poor performance". Follow through on assignments to completion.

13. Understand the principle of personal accountability for yourself and others. Require it of those who accept responsibility for various ministries in your congregation. People are inspired to perform at their highest level when they know they will be held accountable.

14. Understand the importance of working together as it relates to the eldership. God's infinite wisdom was at work in requiring a plurality of elders in local congregations. Strive for win/win agreements within the eldership where every final decision is always fully supported by every elder.

15. Learn how to be humble while exhibiting the courage of your convictions as you stand for the truth of God's Word. Never be

overbearing with the congregation, but be confident so that your members will trust your leadership.

The remaining chapters will deal with the practical application of the Bible's timeless principles to effectively accomplish the many works involved in leading your congregation.

CHAPTER FOUR

Church Discipline
Luke 15:4-5

After much contemplation, I decided to begin our discussion on congregational ministries with church discipline. First, because of the vital nature of this work and second, because so many congregations of the Lord's church either do not practice this holy command or do not take this work seriously. Elders must keep in mind the Hebrew writer's instruction that they are to watch for the souls of their flock and that they will ultimately be held accountable for those souls (Hebrews 13:17). The two-fold purpose of church discipline is directly related to that admonition, in that it motivates elders to maintain the spiritual purity of the church, and to bring back wavering souls.

Since there should be no question as to the scriptural authority for church discipline, I will concentrate this discussion on the practical application of these Holy Spirit inspired commands (Romans 16:17; 1 Corinthians 5:4-6; Galatians 6:1,2,9,10; II Thessalonians 3:6,14,15; James 5:19,20). Elders often find this ministry to be the most difficult to administer. That should not, however, be an excuse to disregard the above teaching on this important scriptural task.

The information provided should be considered a guide that can be modified to fit particular circumstances within your congregation. Although there should be consistency in application of Bible principles, there is latitude in this area to adapt to individual circumstances. The timetable for disciplinary action would not be the same for a babe in Christ who is attempting to separate himself/herself from worldly habits versus a mature Christian who knows the way of righteousness but turns away from it (2 Peter 2:21-22).

In order to keep this difficult but critical work on the front burner of the elders' agenda, it should be discussed at the opening of your weekly meetings. Although there are numerous reasons for initiating disciplinary action with a member, most involve, directly or indirectly, a lack of faithfulness in attending worship services. This ministry work begins with the development of a tracking system that will accurately record the attendance of each adult member of the congregation. This may be done by use of attendance cards, sign-in sheets or head counts in smaller congregations. Someone would then record the results in a format for use by the elders. Exhibit 3 is a simple excel spreadsheet that allows the elders to review at a glance those members who have not been attending Sunday morning or evening services. Those members that have missed services for two or more weeks in a row should be discussed at the elders' weekly meeting and visit or call assignments made as determined by the elder over delinquents. As the old saying goes "an ounce of prevention is better than a pound of cure." The odds of restoring a weak member are much higher if efforts are started in the early stages of the problem.

Although individual circumstances may dictate otherwise, I recommend that written contact be made after an individual or family has missed two consecutive Sundays. Exhibit 4 is a sample letter simply noting their absence. If there is no response or attendance the next Sunday a second letter is sent and a visit or call is assigned to an elder or preacher (Exhibit 5). If there is no response or attendance on the fourth Sunday, another letter is sent (Exhibit 6) and another visit is assigned. If there is no response or attendance on the fifth Sunday, their name(s) are placed before the congregation on a Sunday or Wednesday night asking members to contact the person(s) and pray for their return (Exhibit 7). One week is given for the delinquent member to respond. If there is no response or attendance, fellowship is formally withdrawn (Exhibit 8) and a letter sent notifying the disfellowshipped member of the congregation's action (Exhibit 9). Periodically, follow up letters are sent and contact is attempted depending on the circumstances (Exhibit 10). To ensure that all members are aware of action taken to disfellowship an erring brother or sister in Christ and their scriptural responsibilities toward that person, a letter should be sent concerning this action (Exhibit 11).

In order to ensure that the congregation understands the scriptural authority and command to practice church discipline, it is vitally important that periodic lessons/sermons are presented explaining the duty. Exhibit 12 contains a lesson outline on this critical subject. I would also recommend at least one sermon a year be presented on church discipline to help instruct the members on this vital work and to demonstrate the preacher's public support of the elders' efforts.

Elders walk a fine line in this ministry between being longsuffering and standing firm in protecting their flock (Galatians 6:1,2,9-10; 2 Thessalonians 3:6). I have worked with the process just discussed and experienced positive results for the erring and the Lord's church. It provides consistent guidelines that are also flexible so that they can be adapted to any situation.

It is my prayer that all elders will accept their God given responsibility to do all they can to bring the erring back to the fold and to protect the flock from sin by practicing Bible instructed church discipline.

CHAPTER FIVE

Deacons
Acts 6:2-4

The apostles understood the need to appoint men to serve under their oversight so that they could concentrate their efforts on spiritual matters.

Although deacons have no specific scriptural authority over a congregation, they play a critical role in the long term success of a flock in carrying out God's mission for the church. Most elders were previously deacons at their congregations. Occasionally, elders are appointed that were not deacons, but as we all know, this is not the norm. We discussed developing leaders in Chapter Two to include the use of the matrix in Exhibit 1 as a guide to ensure the continual progress of potential leaders in the development of their leadership skills and qualifications. This chapter will deal with the practical aspects of the office of deacon.

Developing Deacons

This process begins by observing the men of your congregation as they worship, serve, lead their families, and interact with other members and the public. Identify those men that show leadership potential. Their wives and children also play an important role in the qualification process (1 Timothy 3:8-13). Provide these men opportunities to be tested with assignments in various ministries. You should then observe their performance of these duties. Are they dependable, thorough, and self-motivated? Do they work well with others, accept direction and constructive criticism and grow in the work? As a family do they meet the qualifications for this work? Appointing deacons is serious business and should never be taken lightly.

As the need arises, schedule a prospective deacon's class on a Wednesday night or Sunday morning for part or all of a quarter. This class should be taught by the elders with possible help from the preacher and/or current deacons. Elders should invite those they have identified as potential leaders (rifle approach) and then open the class up to all men in the congregation. A sample invitation letter and curriculum is shown as Exhibit 13.

Once you identify a specific need for additional deacon(s), and men who exhibit the desire and appear to meet the qualifications, it is time to schedule separate meetings between the elders and the men and their spouses, to begin serious discussions about becoming deacons. Exhibit 14 is a discussion outline that can be modified to fit your individual needs.

One of the goals of the development process is to eliminate as many surprises as possible after a man is appointed a deacon. The elders must ensure that every prospect is scripturally sound and that he believes in and maintains high moral standards for himself and his family. They must have assurances that a prospective deacon will support the elders and the various ministries of their congregation. Exhibit 15 is a questionnaire for prospective deacons, teachers, preachers, guest speakers, and short and long term missionaries associated with your congregation. The answers will reveal positions on various doctrinal subjects that may merit further discussion or withdrawal of the prospect's consideration for the positions just mentioned. This questionnaire may seem harsh, but failure to be pro-active in the development of qualified leaders in the Lord's church is rarely the best course of action in the long run.

Once the questionnaire is reviewed and any issues resolved to everyone's satisfaction, the prospective deacons should be asked to read and complete a commitment questionnaire (Exhibit 16). Accountability is one of the greatest motivators. Completing this questionnaire establishes a written understanding of their expected responsibilities. This process should be repeated every year during the annual review of each deacon's ministry work.

Now that the preparation work has been completed, the elders can nominate prospective deacons with confidence that the congregation will approve of their appointment. Exhibit 17 provides sample procedures for placing a man's name before the congregation for their consideration.

If there are no substantiated objections to these men, the elders can now proceed with their appointments. Exhibit 18 provides sample procedures for the installation of deacons.

Overseeing Deacons

Exhibit 19 contains elder/deacon assignments that should be updated as changes occur. This list provides the elders, deacons and office staff accurate information on the primary responsibilities of the congregation's leaders.

As you will note on this form, individual elders have primary responsibility over various ministries within the congregation. This *does not* mean that these ministries are not under the oversight of the entire eldership. It is simply a leadership tool that will promote increased effectiveness in carrying out the work of individual ministries. Deacons do not need to coordinate with the entire eldership on routine decisions nor should they get mixed signals from various elders on how to proceed with their work. Individual elders are responsible for informing the eldership of routine decisions made within each ministry. Major actions or decisions should be discussed by the eldership prior to implementation by a deacon.

To ensure effective performance by your deacons, each ministry should have a written description that clearly states its objectives and responsibilities. These should be developed with the current deacons' input to help create a sense of ownership in these works. Elders should review ministry descriptions with newly appointed deacons to eliminate any misunderstandings about their responsibilities. Sample descriptions are provided in Exhibit 20.

We know that the church has a responsibility to care for the widows and elderly, particularly the shut-ins. If this work is assigned to your deacons, then guidelines and reporting procedures should be established to ensure effective accomplishment of these efforts. Sample guidelines are provided in Exhibit 21. It is recommended that deacons report on their monthly visit during scheduled meetings with the elders. The deacon can also in addition to/or instead of, submit to their primary elder a simple report form which contains such information as: the deacon's and widow's name, date of visit, routine work done and any pertinent information the elders should know.

It is strongly recommended that elder/deacon meetings be scheduled monthly. The deacons can meet among themselves to discuss their ministries and develop agenda items for the elders meeting that would immediately follow. During the combined meeting, the elders should ask each deacon specific questions about his ministry, widow/elderly visit, etc. Again, public accountability is an effective motivator to ensure performance. Elders should also use this time to inform the deacons of upcoming events, decisions made by the elders and to enlist their input on various subjects.

An annual meeting between each deacon and his overseeing elder to review the previous year's work and plan for the upcoming year is essential to maintaining the focus and commitment of deacons. This process also strengthens the sense of ownership each deacon must have in his ministry in order to be successful in carrying out God's work in his area.

Annual deacon retreats are also a planning tool that strengthens all ministries and helps to build relationships among the deacons. These meetings can comprise a weekend at a location away from town that may include the wives and children or simply a Saturday meeting at the church building. A sample meeting agenda is provided in Exhibit 22 that includes elder provided topics, old business from last year's meeting, and individual ministry reports.

In order for deacons to be most successful in carrying out their assigned responsibilities, the elder primarily responsible for that specific work must show personal interest in that work and maintain continual communication with the deacon. A balance should be struck between too much and too little oversight of their efforts based on individual circumstances. As new deacons grow in competence, the need for strict oversight diminishes, thereby freeing up more of the elders' precious time. Competent deacons should enjoy the relative freedom to carry out their ministry responsibilities with minimal oversight by the elder responsible for that work.

CHAPTER SIX

Foreign Evangelism
Romans 10:14-15

P aul emphasizes the importance of congregations sending out qualified people to preach to the lost wherever they may be located.

There should be no question about the need for and responsibility of every local congregation to evangelize the world for Christ (Matthew 9:37,38; 28:19,20). The Lord, in His infinite wisdom, has left the methods of accomplishing this command to us. The challenge for every congregation, large or small, is to develop a balanced approach to mission work that includes local and foreign efforts. The extent of that involvement depends on several factors such as: the size of a congregation, financial resources, manpower, experience, local demographics, etc. This chapter will discuss foreign evangelism with local evangelism being covered in the next chapter.

Supporting or Sponsoring a Missionary

Generally, when a congregation initially decides to become involved in foreign mission work it is by way of supporting or sponsoring a missionary as opposed to overseeing one, as we will discuss later in this chapter. Congregational leaders must first determine the geographical area for their work and the man they wish to support in that area. These decisions must not be taken lightly. Careful and prayerful preparation must be made so that the Lord's resources are invested wisely with a reasonable expectation of productive results. Research should consist of talking to other congregational leaders, missionaries, preaching schools, Christian universities, reading church related periodicals, and attending mission forums to become familiar with on-going missionary efforts. Important factors for a potential area would be the character and receptivity of the native people, their attitudes toward Americans, the religious environment, and status of the government in control. Also research the number of missionaries working that area either in country as residents or through periodic trips from the United States. Consider a survey trip to the area to view firsthand the on-going work of current missionaries.

Determining the area for missionary work is important, but selecting the right family to support that work is critical and requires extensive preparation to ensure that this family would be suitable for your congregational support. There should be an initial meeting with the church leaders where the missionary will explain his credentials by discussing his experience, references, education, selected geographical area covered, results of his efforts, finances, other supporting congregations, family, doctrinal positions, and most importantly his overseeing congregation. Meet with his church leaders, if feasible, to gain knowledge of the extent of their oversight. Ask the prospective missionary, as a minimum the following questions:

1. "Are all supporting funds sent to the overseeing congregation for distribution?"

2. "Do the elders make periodic field trips to observe the missionary's work?"

3. "How often is there communication between the missionary and his overseeing elders?"

4. "Does the missionary provide periodic reports to his supporting congregations?"

5. "Do any of the supporting congregations make short-term mission trips to assist the missionary in his field work?"

6. "Does the missionary come home periodically to personally report to his supporting congregations?"

7. "What are the major doctrinal positions of his overseeing eldership?"

8. "Does the missionary or overseeing elders publish periodic financial statements?"

9. "What commitment has the missionary made as to his length of stay in the field?"

10. "Will the missionary complete a questionnaire on his doctrinal and moral positions?" (Exhibit 15)

If a meeting is not feasible, these questions can be asked and answered by mail or e-mail. Prior to a final decision being made on supporting a missionary, he should make a presentation to your congregation, answer questions, and his family should spend social time with the members. Allow a period after his presentation for members to provide feedback to the elders on their impression of the man, his family, and his work. It is very important that the congregation "take ownership" of this mission effort so that they will support the elders' decision for the congregation's involvement in this work. Encourage them to communicate with the missionary and his wife. Also consider planning a short-term team trip to the mission area to work with the missionary. These trips are extremely effective in building long-term support for involvement in the mission effort. Later in this chapter we will discuss how to plan and effectively execute a short-term mission trip.

Overseeing a Missionary

Accepting the oversight of a missionary family is a major responsibility that requires extensive preparation and continual effort to ensure that this work is done effectively. The congregation must be sure that they have the manpower, experience, expertise, time, financial capacity and long term commitment to foreign evangelism necessary for success. Without these, the work of the Lord in seeking and saving the lost may well suffer long-term harm. As we know, elders will one day answer for their deeds (Hebrews 13:17).

Some years ago, the eldership at my previous congregation interviewed a missionary about joining the work in the Pacific Islands that the elders oversaw. He and his family had recently returned from another overseas area where they had spent three years attempting to establish the church. We asked this man to describe his decision and preparation to enter foreign mission work, his search for an overseeing eldership and the subsequent relationship he had with them during the three years he was working under their oversight. His response broke our hearts.

This man had just graduated from college and the elders he chose to work with had never overseen a foreign missionary. Soon after arriving in the field, after little interaction with his elders, he was asked by another congregation in the same area to "temporarily" fill in for their preacher who had recently returned to the United States. This assignment lasted most of the three years he was in the field. By the time he was able to start evangelizing his planned area of the country, his co-worker decided to return home and he started to lose his financial support. During his time in the field, his overseeing elders never visited him and had very little written or verbal communication with him. The end result of his three years of effort was one baptism and no new congregations established.

There are relatively few men today that are committed to taking the gospel to foreign fields and many congregations that may not know how to actively support and/or oversee this work. The church must be prepared to take on this holy responsibility (Matthew 9:37,38; 28:19,20). It is impossible to fully discuss this important task in the space available here, but I will recommend a useful process for selecting an overseas area, selecting missionaries, preparing missionaries, ongoing oversight of the missionary, selecting an eldership and developing and maintaining congregational support and commitment for foreign evangelism.

Selecting the Area – As previously mentioned, important factors in the selection process are the character and receptivity of the native people, their attitudes toward Americans and Christianity, the type and stability of the local government, the economy, health care, security, cost of living, schools, transportation and current missionary efforts in the area. Research and discussions with people such as current or former missionaries, Christian college professors, etc., who know the areas being considered are also critical in making an informed decision.

Selecting the Missionary – Your number one concern should be doctrinal soundness (2 Timothy 1:13). That can be determined by a questionnaire (Exhibit 15), interviews and contact with previous congregations, current or former missionaries, preaching schools or Christian universities he attended. The prospect should be married with strong family support. Marriage is not an absolute requirement, but a wife provides important spiritual and social support to a missionary in his work. He must display strong interpersonal skills, a positive attitude, versatility, self-motivation and the ability to organize and cope with adversity (Romans 5:1-4). He must have a true love for lost souls, a willingness to study God's Word, and spiritual maturity (2 Timothy 2:15). He must have strong Bible knowledge and be in good mental and physical health. He must be humble and adaptable. He must be committed to the work and respect the authority of the elders and their method of oversight (Hebrews 13:17). He must be spiritually and emotionally mature, financially responsible, trustworthy and experienced in evangelizing the lost (I Corinthians 4:2; Philippians 2:19,22; Hebrews 5:12-14).

Seek candidates through recommendations from missionaries you currently support, other missionaries, preaching schools, Christian universities, and supporting congregations.

Prior to interviewing a candidate, ask them to complete a questionnaire (Exhibit 15) to help you understand their doctrinal and moral positions. The first meeting should be an informal one with the husband and wife. The elders should then determine if a second meeting is worthwhile based on the answers to the questionnaire and information and impressions obtained during the first meeting. The next meeting should be a detailed discussion of all facets of the work: a survey trip, finances (a requirement for emergency evacuation funds, retirement account and medical insurance are strongly recommended), oversight, work plan, time tables, etc. The man and his wife should then make a survey trip to the selected mission field. Upon their return, both parties will then make a final decision as to their commitment to continue the preparation process. The elders and missionary should at this time sign a Terms of Oversight Agreement so that there are no misunderstandings concerning vacations or termination of the relationship (Exhibit 23). It is not recommended that strict written performance requirements be developed due to the nature of the work. The elders will determine adequate levels of effort through newsletters, financial reports, visits to the field every other year and face to face meetings with the missionary during his trips back to the United States.

Preparing the Missionary – It would be ideal for this missionary family to move to your congregation for at least one year in order to develop a sound working relationship with the elders and congregation. During this time they will be raising support and making other preparations for the mission field. They will first develop a work plan that includes short and long-term goals, strategies for accomplishing those goals, and a financial plan. Spiritual preparation includes daily Bible study, development of first principles lessons on such topics as the inspiration of the Bible, the one church, plan of salvation, etc. for use in the field and periodic local teaching and preaching. Financial preparation would consist of developing an informational packet for potential supporting individuals and congregations, a PowerPoint presentation, DVD and list of potential supporting congregations. Travel by the missionary and his family to visit potential supporters should be a continual process throughout this time to ensure that adequate one-time and monthly financial support is secured. The elders can assist with these visits when appropriate in order to provide information to potential elderships on the work and extent of oversight. Cultural preparation should include a study of the history and culture of the country(s) in which he will work, reading material on mission work and contact with current missionaries. Depending on the climate and extent and type of travel required in the mission area, physical preparation may be necessary. Interpersonal preparation includes office hours at your building, assisting your local preacher with visits and Bible studies, frequent meetings with the elders and family participation in various congregational social activities. Informal monthly meetings with the missionary's primary elder are an important part of his preparation. All of the above will contribute to the goal of building a trusting relationship with the congregation in general and the elders in particular.

Ongoing oversight of the Missionary – If your congregation is going to oversee (not sponsor) a missionary then it is recommended that all financial support be sent to you and deposited into a general checking account from which it will be disbursed each month into the missionary's work, salary and special projects checking accounts, based on his budget. Routine continuous expenses such as housing, travel, publications, insurance, vehicle maintenance, etc. would be paid from the work account. Unique expenses such as mission field benevolence, family medical travel, family member evacuation, and major vehicle or home mechanical system replacement would be paid with funds from the special projects account. Funds for the relocation of his family and possessions when the missionary returns to live in the United States would also be maintained in this account. He would have independent access to his work and salary accounts but not the special projects account. Coordination with the overseeing elders would be required before funds are transferred from the special projects account into his work account. This process, in addition to monthly financial statements regarding income and expenditures to and from his work account, provide the overseeing elders and the missionary's supporting congregations reasonable assurance of accountability for all funds associated with supporting the work. The electronic funds transfer (EFT) process between accounts ensures immediate availability of special project funds. Although not mandatory, monthly contributions to an IRA or Roth IRA retirement account is strongly recommended as a condition of oversight, as is family medical insurance regardless of the medical coverage available from the host country. These requirements help to provide fiscal and physical protection of the missionary family's future as well as alleviating the supporting congregations of much of the potential financial burden for unforeseen events. It is a good idea for the missionary to write a monthly newsletter to all supporters as well as maintain continual e-mail and phone contact with the elders, generally through his primary elder, to keep everyone involved and up to date on his activities in the mission field. I recommend that an elder and his wife visit the missionary family in the field bi-annually to encourage them, evaluate their work, and provide insight and suggestions. That elder would then report back to the overseeing eldership. These trips should be funded by the missionary. The missionary and his family should return to the United States bi-annually in the years opposite the elders' field visits to report to their supporting congregations and confirm/raise financial support. Supporting congregations can provide short term missionary teams by encouraging individual members to make trips into the field to work with the missionary. These individuals would complete a questionnaire (Exhibit 15) and agree to work under the direction of the missionary in the field. I will discuss short term group campaigns later in this chapter.

Selecting an Eldership – In many respects the elder – missionary relationship is a "two way street." The prospective missionary must be assured that his overseeing eldership is doctrinally sound (Titus 1:9). Past experience in sponsoring or overseeing a missionary is highly desirable, but not absolutely necessary as long as the elders are willing to seek advice (Romans 10:2; Proverbs 16:18). They should be personally committed to foreign evangelism and willing to provide a substantial portion of the missionary's financial support (Romans 10:14,15). They should be trustworthy and courageous (Deuteronomy 31:7,8). Oversight should include periodic field visits for the reasons previously mentioned. Items such as reporting requirements, work agreement, and congregational support should be discussed early in the decision making process. The elders should be willing to provide direction and correction, as well as being prepared to deal with emergencies.

Developing and Maintaining Congregational Commitment – Elders and missionaries cannot "rest on their laurels" once a decision has been made to oversee a foreign work. If the congregation loses interest in this area, the work will undoubtedly suffer. The missionary's family activity during the preparatory year with the local congregation is critically important in solidifying the congregation's support. The elders should continually show visible involvement, support, and promotion of this work. This can be achieved by encouraging sermons, reports, and bulletin board information that bring awareness to the mission work.

Short-Term Missionary Campaigns – Short-term campaigns have the potential to strengthen the Lord's work in foreign countries, encourage the resident missionary and his family, and promote support for foreign evangelism at local congregations in the United States. These trips must be carefully planned and executed. If they are not, there is also potential for harming the Lord's work both locally and in foreign fields. In the remainder of this chapter, we will discuss the planning, preparation, and execution of a successful short-term mission trip.

1. *Long Term Planning* – Due to the extensive preparation necessary to ensure the successful outcome of a short-term campaign, it is advised that planning should begin at least two years in advance. The first decisions concern the site, purpose of the trip and selection of a team leader with prior campaign experience and a dependable assistant who has exhibited leadership potential. The team leader will work closely with the missionary and be responsible for overseeing the preparation and execution of the campaign. Usually the missionary will offer several recommendations for consideration. He may see a need to plant the church in a new area or city; strengthen a congregation through Bible Classes; assist with local evangelism to help grow a congregation; or provide in-depth classes on a specific subject matter. Next a determination would be made as to the number and type of people required for this campaign to include the use of men, women, teens, seniors, couples, etc. The cost to each member, the amount the church may be able to contribute and possible fund raising options should be considered. Research should be done to determine modes of travel and any restrictions such as weight or number of pieces of luggage. Local conditions such as availability of lodging, transportation, food, health care, disease and government must also be determined. Before setting a date, the elders should take into account local weather, flight availability, and the academic calendar in the United States for children, teens or college age members who wish to participate. A training schedule should be developed to ensure that all participants are fully prepared for the work to be done. Finally a timetable should be established, starting with dates to announce the campaign to the congregation and a schedule for training classes to ensure adequate preparation prior to the campaign dates.

2. *Initial Meeting* – Training classes should start about eighteen months prior to the campaign. The first meeting should be attended by any members who are curious about this effort. The primary purpose of this meeting will be to explain the goal of the campaign. The structure and activities at the monthly meetings will be dictated by the goal of the campaign, but the general purpose of

these meetings will be to train, prepare, and unify the group. The first meeting will also cover the following subjects: destination, time frames (time of year and duration of the trip), transportation, personnel requirements/restrictions (teen policy regarding on-site adult responsibility), training schedule, teaching aids, financial requirements, appointment of a secretary, insurance (medical/trip), passport and visas, immunizations, and overview of the area to be visited (local culture, customs, conditions, religions, etc). See Exhibit 25

3. *Monthly Training Meetings* – The appointed secretary would maintain attendance records and prepare the minutes from each meeting and distribute them at the beginning of the next meeting. The team leader or his assistant will review the previous meeting minutes at the start of each meeting. Use of correspondence courses is an excellent method to develop interest in a new area of work. The missionary can run ads in local papers or on the radio offering free Bible correspondence courses. Requests for courses can be distributed to team members who will prepare and send the material, grade the completed questions, and send the next course. This will help to develop potential personal Bible study students for each team member prior to entering the foreign field. The missionary should be able to recommend appropriate courses. One-on-one personal Bible study assignments between team members can be made about six months before the campaign to provide them with experience in studying with local prospects. There should be an in-depth study of local religions and their doctrines in light of Bible teaching. The missionary should also discuss customs to help avoid offending local officials and/or potential converts. Check with the team leader or missionary on any questionable topic or activity. Men can be assigned to present short lessons on personal Bible study topics such as: the inspiration of the Bible, the one church and the conversion process. Each team member should be asked to complete a questionnaire concerning doctrinal issues to provide reasonable assurance that there will be sound teaching by all team members (Exhibit 15). Men and women can be separated and public teaching topics assigned about twelve months out from the campaign. It is important to discuss methods of protecting money and documents while traveling internationally and in the local mission field overseas. Personal safety is also a high priority. Planning for long-term follow up with local prospects should be made to ensure progress will

continue after the team's initial efforts. Three months prior to the campaign, Bible materials may be mailed to a secure site within the target country. A list of specific immunizations obtained from the Center for Disease Control (CDC) or a local infectious disease physician should also be provided at this time. The team leader should assign on-site sermon, devotional, prayer and song leading assignments as well as a daily schedule of activities during the campaign. Team members should notify all their students within one or two months of the campaign about the dates they will arrive, the location of their lodging and times of general activities such as worship services, class times, etc.

4. *Preparation* - Finances are a critical component of campaigns. It is recommended that the local congregation establish a general campaign checking account so that team members can make periodic deposits as they attain personal or outside funds for their trip. The elders should establish policies concerning soliciting contributions from local congregation members and other congregations. The team leader will provide information covering passports, visas, tickets, lodging reservations/roommate assignments, immunizations, health and trip insurance, speaking permits, and packing checklists (Exhibit 24). When making airline arrangements allow extra time between flights to cover unforeseen delays. Prior to arrival, the missionary should make on-site preparations.

5. *Departure* – Team members should be provided a last minute "critical item" checklist from the items listed in Exhibit 24. Allow extra check-in time to deal with unforeseen events.

6. *Arrival* – The team leader/missionary will ensure that team members are prepared for the customs process to include completion of appropriate forms and possible inspection of luggage and that transportation is available upon arrival. Depending on the length of the flights and time changes, allow the team a day to recover from the jet lag, if necessary, before commencing activities. Local notices of arrival should be mailed the first day to all correspondence course students.

7. *On-site Activities* – Begin each day with a team meeting after breakfast. The agenda can include the following:

   • Opening prayer

- Short devotional

- General comments and question and answer session by team leader/missionary

- Team members can discuss the previous day's activities, the status of personal Bible studies, plans for that day, and miscellaneous comments/suggestions.

If the campaign goal is to plant a congregation or create numerical growth in an existing congregation through local evangelism, the daily routines would be similar.

a. Make contact with correspondence course students by phone or in person and attempt to set up personal Bible studies.

b. Attempt to set up personal Bible studies with people at the hotel, restaurants, or others with whom there is repeated contact.

c. Pass out literature in public areas and/or door knocking in neighborhoods (team leader must assure that this activity is allowed by local law and/or custom). Ensure the team leader is aware of each member's location if they are traveling outside the local area of the lodging facility. As a general rule, do not travel alone.

If the campaign goal is to edify a local congregation, attempt to schedule Bible studies on various subjects relating to that goal. These may be done at the hotel or in someone's home. Activities listed in a-c above can be planned and executed as time permits.

Evening activities may include group viewing of DVD's (Jule Miller), question and answer sessions, classes for men, women, children, and teens on various subjects appropriate to the campaign goal. Participants for Sunday worship should be scheduled beforehand along with arrangements for the location, seating, and power (if available).

If a follow up team is coming to reinforce your work, a team meeting should be held to discuss the transition of activities to ensure a seamless handoff. A pre-departure meeting should be held to discuss clearing the hotel, transportation to the airport, and procedures to include necessary documentation, money conversion, and tickets.

Finally, schedule an "after trip" meeting within two weeks of return to discuss lessons learned. Preparation and execution procedures can be updated based on the trip's experiences. Exhibit 25 is an outline of the process discussed above.

As you have just read, foreign evangelism requires a substantial investment in time, effort and money. The rewards for work well-planned and executed are well worth the investment. The fields are white with harvest in many countries and God expects His children to make every effort to reach the lost in all the world.

CHAPTER SEVEN

Local Evangelism
Mark 12:30-31

Christ teaches us that the two greatest commandments are to love God and love our neighbors. We demonstrate that love for our neighbors by reaching out to them with the saving gospel of Christ.

My wife and I built a previous home on a piece of property filled with large trees. We were very careful with the site preparation in order to leave as many trees as possible so that we could enjoy their beauty and shade for many years to come. After 2-3 years, we noticed three of these trees were dying. My brother, who is in the tree service business, remarked that not only were those trees dying but several others were showing early signs of problems. He explained that during the site preparation the heavy earth moving equipment had damaged the root systems of the remaining trees. Also, dirt had covered the bases of the trees during construction thus preventing life giving nutrients from reaching the tops of these trees. I walked the yard admiring the foliage, but was saddened by the realization that the condition of the base and root systems of the trees were ultimately going to cause the loss of much of this beauty. Had I paid attention to these issues during the clearing of the property, the loss might have been avoided.

You may be asking, "What in the world do these trees have to do with local evangelism?" The answer is "everything." It is human nature to gravitate toward those activities that we enjoy and are good at doing. Foreign evangelism is exciting and requires little direct involvement by local members of a congregation that support or even oversee a missionary. We often receive monthly reports of the work and periodic presentations of success in foreign lands that are exciting and uplifting. As you will read throughout this book, balance is the key to the overall success of a congregation in carrying out the Lord's work. If the same effort and emphasis is not placed on local evangelism (the root system) as on foreign evangelism (foliage at the top) then the spiritual, numerical, and financial health of the congregation will be in jeopardy. Most members, and often the elders, deacons and preachers, are not overly excited about local evangelism for various reasons. They know there is a need for it, but shy away from involvement because it often requires direct contact with friends, relatives, neighbors, visitors, and strangers to discuss religion.

In order to overcome this natural tendency in most of us, a structured program should be developed that will facilitate the implementation and continued effective operation of this vital ministry. The critical key to continued success in any ministry, especially this one, is support and promotion by the leadership of a congregation. As mentioned earlier, the elders "set the bar" when it comes to commitment to any work of the church. They must be involved in the development and implementation of this program and continually promote it publicly and privately. They must also ensure that the right person is assigned to oversee the daily work. This designation will assign direct responsibility to an individual thus promoting accountability for success. It may be a preacher, deacon, or qualified member who has the needed organizational, motivational, and people skills. In addition to a strong local outreach program, I highly recommend that a personal evangelism class be conducted for the adults and teens at least annually in order to build confidence and provide your members with the tools to teach the lost. This class can be taught by the preacher, an elder, or other qualified member. Sound effective material is available from various sources.[9]

Many books have been written about local evangelism. It is not my intent to present an in-depth study of this subject, but to provide examples of proven programs for your consideration. There are numerous local outreach programs available for use by congregations. Careful consideration should be given as to which program would work best for your congregation.

Fishers of Men – This ministry is an intensive twelve-week course of specialized training in person-to-person evangelism conducted by full or part-time instructors trained in this program. There are eleven two and one half hour classes for eleven consecutive weeks with weekly homework plus Bible studies with non-Christians. Since 1977, there have been over 18,000 baptisms resulting from 100 instructors teaching over 1,000 courses to 16,000 members of the church in 950 congregations.[10]

Monday Night for the Master – This program was developed by Gary Bodine in the 1990's in Texas. I have personally known of three congregations that have successfully implemented this program or a variation of it as part of their local outreach ministry. Members meet every Monday night for a meal (optional) before making calls, sending cards, making visits, or conducting Bible Studies with current members and recent visitors. Members specify their interests and talents from preparing food, clean-up, babysitting, visiting, card writing, calling, and Bible studies. This program has something for everyone.[11]

Generic Local Outreach Program – This program consists of a primary elder or congregational leader that is responsible for local outreach. There would be a deacon or qualified man assigned as local outreach coordinator, and five other deacons or responsible men assigned as team leaders for each of the five major areas of the program:

1. Visitors – Worship
2. Visitors – Follow-up
3. Community Involvement
4. Promotion
5. Bible Studies

Their responsibilities are as follows:

Worship Team Leader Responsibilities:

1. Coordinate with the primary elder, local outreach coordinator, and local outreach program team leaders of the selection of team members.

2. Schedule 4 team members to greet visitors each Sunday morning and evening (2 couples/4 individuals or combination).

3. Schedule team members to check pews each Sunday morning for attendance cards and sharpened pencils.

4. Oversee the following activities each Sunday:

   a. Visitors are greeted.
   b. Attendance cards/pencils are in place.
   c. Ensure late arrivals complete attendance cards.
   d. Deacons are at assigned doors at the end of services.
   e. Visitors are invited to lunch.

5. Publish visitor's names/phone numbers in the following Sunday's bulletin so members can personally thank them for visiting.

6. Provide weekly report to the local outreach coordinator and follow-up team leader each Sunday (Exhibit 26).

7. Coordinate with follow-up team leader to ensure all visitors are contacted.

8. Meet monthly with the local outreach coordinator and other team leaders to discuss the local outreach program.

9. Meet with the local outreach team annually to assess program performance and review short and long term goals if necessary.

10. Short term goals – procedures, team members in place by (date): program active by (date).

11. Long term goal – 100% of visitors greeted, invited to lunch and contacted each Sunday.

Follow-up Team Leader Responsibilities:

1. Coordinate with primary elder, local outreach coordinator, and local outreach program team leaders on selection of team members.

2. Schedule visitor phone callers each week (4 men/women).

3. Provide visitor names to callers.

4. Coordinate with elders on Monday night visitation schedule.

5. Ensure office staff has visitor list in order to send information packet (DVD, elder/preacher letter, brochure, Bible material, etc.).

6. Ensure door hangers (visitor, sick/shut-in, delinquent) are printed and available.

7. Provide names/addresses to Bible class teachers by Wednesday night for note writing by students.

8. Ensure the visitation team coordinator receives visitor cards by Monday.

9. Collect contact reports by Wednesday night (Exhibit 27).

10. Provide weekly report to local outreach coordinator each Sunday.

11. Coordinate with worship team leader, visitation coordinator, and Bible study team leader to ensure follow-up.

12. Maintain automated record of each visitor.

13. Attend monthly meeting with local outreach coordinator and other team members to discuss local outreach program.

14. Meet with local outreach coordinator annually to review program performance and review/revise short and long term goals if necessary.

15. Short term goals - procedures, team members in place by (date); program active by (date).

16. Long term goals – 100% of Sunday visitors will be called, sent a welcome packet, visited by an elder or visitation team member and invited to study the Bible.

Community Involvement Team Leader Responsibilities:

1. Coordinate with primary elder, local outreach coordinator and local outreach program team leaders on selection of team members.

2. Develop contacts with appropriate agencies within the various communities to utilize as sources for finding needy families.

3. chedule and implement periodic visits to area nursing homes.

4. Schedule and implement periodic blood drives.

5. Contact families of prisoners involved in the prison ministry.

6. Utilize senior's group as a tool for local outreach through their friends and associations.

7. Coordinate with the elder responsible for gospel meetings to schedule seminars on such topics as family, drugs, and crime prevention to attract concerned citizens.

8. Coordinate with area congregations to establish a central warehouse for clothing and possibly furniture to be used to assist needy families.

9. Provide local outreach coordinator a monthly report on scheduled activities, activities in progress, and activities completed by the first

of each month (Exhibit 28).

10. Coordinate with the Bible study team leader on possible leads for studies.

11. Attend monthly team meetings with local outreach coordinator and other team leaders to discuss the local outreach program. Meet with local outreach coordinator annually to review the program performance and review/revise short and long range goals if necessary.

12. Short term goals – Operating procedures in place by (date), team members selected by (date), program active by (date).

13. Long term goals – Continual involvement in local community benevolent activities; provide continuing leads to Bible study team leader through interaction with local community government benevolent/social activities and residents; increase visitors at worship services through continual interaction with local community government benevolent/social activities and residents.

Promotion Team Leader Responsibilities:

1. Coordinate with primary elder, local outreach coordinator and local outreach program team leaders on selection of team members.

2. Look into possibility of directional signs at appropriate intersections in the local area.

3. Study possibility of an advertising sign adjacent to a main road.

4. Ensure development and production of generic church business cards, calendars, and quick-read tracts that promote the congregation and doctrine.

5. Ensure building sign is changed weekly and is used primarily to promote local outreach.

6. Develop and price an ad for the elders' consideration.

7. Ensure that ads are placed in local newspapers for various local outreach functions such as VBS, seminars, gospel meetings and forums.

8. Ensure periodic local mailings of promotional materials.

9. Write articles on local evangelism for your bulletin.

10. Create/update church website to emphasize local outreach by providing information of interest to the community (directions to building, contact information, programs for children, singles, seniors, and seminars on topics of local interest).

11. Explore the feasibility of hosting a local outreach forum for area congregations.

12. Attend monthly meeting with local outreach coordinator and other team leaders to discuss the local outreach program.

13. Meet annually with the local outreach coordinator to review program performance and review/revise short and long-range goals if necessary.

14. Short term goals – Operating procedures in place by (date), team members selected and program active by (date).

15. Long term goals – Increase the local visibility of the congregation and its various activities.

Bible Study Team Leader Responsibilities:

1. Coordinate with primary elder, local outreach coordinator and local outreach program team leaders on selection of team members. Members must be capable of conducting basic Bible studies.

2. Ensure the continued viability of the Bible correspondence course program by continual review of material, processing of requests for courses, the grading and return of tests and personal follow up when appropriate.

3. Ensure the continued viability of the prison ministry through continual review of the scheduling of visits, study material, and recruitment of new teachers.

4. Coordinate with the elders on the development of periodic personal evangelism classes.

5. Ensure the continual availability of qualified Bible study teachers by thorough training and recruitment.

6. Ensure every effort is made to continue Bible studies that are

initiated until students are baptized and grounded.

7. Short term goals – Operating procedures in place by (date); team members selected and program active by (date).

8. Long term goals – The congregation is always prepared to teach God's word at every opportunity.

* *Building and Grounds* – You may ask what in the world do building and grounds have to do with local evangelism? The answer is plenty! Your congregation has just one opportunity to make a good first impression on visitors. The condition of your building and grounds will send a positive or negative message to approaching visitors about the care you have as stewards of the Lord's resources. The appearance of the foyer/entryway and restrooms are often the first interior area visitors see. Are these areas clean, orderly and appealing to the eye? Is the auditorium clean, organized, and fully stocked with bibles, song books, attendance cards, and pens? If you neglect these areas you may well lose visitors before they sit down for worship.

Conclusion – If we are to be pleasing to the Lord as a congregation of the Lord's people, we must have an effective local outreach program (Luke 19:10). This work should not be left to the preacher(s). It is God's plan that everyone should be involved in reaching the lost, and it is the elders' responsibility to develop and implement a program that involves as many members as possible. An effective local outreach ministry is as important as any work of the local congregation. Plan the work and work the plan! See the organizational chart at Exhibit 70.

CHAPTER EIGHT

Involvement
1 Corinthians 12:12-27

Paul teaches us the importance of every member of the body of Christ using their unique talents to strengthen the Lord's church.

This chapter follows our discussion on local evangelism because local outreach and involvement will result in *sustained* spiritual and numerical growth in a congregation. Growth cannot be sustained without an effective involvement program. We must use our members or we will lose them. While local outreach opens the front door to our congregations, involvement closes the back door by keeping members engaged in the work of the church. An effective involvement ministry will help believers become fruitful and fulfilled in meaningful areas of service.

The various programs discussed in this chapter are for possible use in your congregation depending on the individual resources and needs unique to your situation. They can easily be modified to be productive on a smaller scale. It is also anticipated that they will spur ideas for similar programs that may be better suited for your congregation. Please keep in mind that although these programs may seem complex and time consuming upon a first read, once these activities are up and running, my experience has shown that the effort necessary to be effective is not overwhelming. Individuals can easily participate as members and leaders in multiple programs.

We all know that it is much harder to attract new members than it is to keep current ones. When members choose to leave a congregation the reasons given for leaving are often: "I never felt appreciated;" "No one seemed to care if I was there or not;" and "I'm not needed, no one ever asked me to serve." These reasons can be easily eliminated with an effective involvement program that is overseen by a deacon or mature Christian with good organizational and motivational skills.

Member Information – When Christians place membership, ask them to promptly complete an information form containing the following data on themselves and their family: full names, address, phone numbers (home/ cell/work), emergency contact(s), e-mail addresses, employer, occupation, date of birth, marital status, spouse, anniversary date, baptism date, last congregation attended (city/state). Information on children living at home should include: names, dates of birth and date of baptism, if baptized.

New Members Orientation Class – This class can be held on a periodic or "as needed" basis depending on the circumstances at individual congregations. It is recommended that the class be taught by the elders or mature men in the congregation if there are no elders. This is a good time for new members to become personally acquainted with these congregational leaders. It is imperative that new members quickly learn about the doctrinal positions and various ministries of their congregation so that they can begin the spiritual, social, and ministry assimilation process necessary to ground them in the congregation. See Exhibit 29 for class outline.

Satan is watching how we care for new members of our congregation. If he sees that they are not being assimilated spiritually, socially, and through ministry involvement, he is going to attack them in an attempt to pull them back into the world. As just mentioned, the keys to ensuring new members do not fall away in the early stages of membership are through the following actions:

- Spiritual growth through appropriate Bible classes. Classes and personal studies can be determined during the new members' orientation.

- Social growth through Life Group sponsors who work with new members to help them meet and develop social relationships with other members. The church office can assign new members to a Life Group where the group leader has responsibility for social assimilation. Smaller congregations can accomplish this function through an elder, deacon, or designated family.

- Involvement in ministries in which they have interest and talents. Providing practical ways to involve members in ministries they enjoy and can apply their talents will create a "sense of ownership" in those ministries thus ensuring their continued commitment and reducing potential "burn out." *To sustain a successful involvement program, it must be interest/talent based and not needs based.* How many times have the following questions been asked without giving thought to the member's interest or talent in these areas: "Joe, we need a Bible School Director, will you do it?", or "Mary, we need a primary class teacher, will you do it?"

Ministry involvement – This starts with prompt completion of an involvement profile that will provide the involvement coordinator with the information he needs to utilize new members in areas of service which they will enjoy and excel. If profiles are not currently being used, it is recommended that all members complete one as soon as possible in order to formalize this process throughout the congregation. This can be done quickly by taking one Sunday Bible class hour to have all members in attendance complete a profile. Leaders can answer any questions and provide explanations during that time. Absent members can be contacted by ministry leaders to complete their profiles. The data should then be entered into an automated program (such as Excel), so that information can be quickly obtained when help is needed in a particular ministry. An example of a generic profile is shown in Exhibit 30. Once this effort is completed, it will be easy to identify those members who are not actively involved in any ministry of the congregation. These people can be targeted for personal contact by congregational leaders to encourage them to be more involved. Sermons on involvement would also be beneficial at this time. I cannot stress strongly enough the critical importance of having the right person over the involvement ministry. All the data in the world will be of little value unless it is utilized to ensure fruitful involvement in the right ministry by each member. This person must work closely with the other ministry leaders to ensure members are being utilized effectively.

Life Groups – When a congregation grows to approximately 30-40 families it becomes more difficult to manage such activities as social events, showers, caring for sick and bereaved and contacting absentees. Dividing the congregation into groups with a nearly equal number of couples, singles, widows, widowers, children, elders, and deacons, will reduce the ministry workload to a manageable level and help to ensure that the social and physical needs of the members are met in an effective manner. It is recommended that a deacon or mature member with excellent organizational skills be appointed as coordinator. Each group would have a leader and possibly an assistant leader, who would then appoint activity leaders of such areas as showers, social events, transportation, meals, new members and absentees. These groups should meet on a regular basis to discuss their work and to develop deeper social relationships within the group. The membership of each group could be changed every six to twelve months so that friendships can be strengthened throughout the congregation. These groups in no way diminish the elders' God given responsibility to lead their congregation. The groups are simply a method or tool utilized by the elders to execute their duties in this area effectively.

Life Group Leader Responsibilities

Group leaders would work under the direction of the life group coordinator. This coordinator would report to a specific elder who has primary responsibility for the Involvement ministry, who in turn reports to the eldership on these activities. Major areas could be as follows:

Fellowship – The strongest bond we have to bind us to the work of the church is fellowship. God understood we would be subjected to trials and temptations and therefore provided the bond of fellowship to protect us from the world. Withdrawal of fellowship is the only means we have of showing disapproval of our brethren's actions. Therefore, positive acts of fellowship are vital to the well-being of all Christians. The fellowship that occurs naturally when the body comes together should be supported by special social gatherings or planned activities, in addition to regular worship services where members can develop deeper relationships with each other. New group members, especially converts, should be contacted quickly to start assimilating them into the congregation. They should be introduced to other members of the group and the congregation and exposed to the various ministries of the church. Special note should be taken of unique needs of any group member, but especially new ones. If these needs cannot be met by the group, this information should be passed on to the group coordinator or elders for action.

Involvement – As previously mentioned, one of the best ways of keeping members is to get them involved in activities suited to their interests and talents. Start by reviewing the new member's involvement profile (Exhibit 30) and the life group profile (Exhibit 32). Also, meet with new members to discuss their interests and fully explain the various activities available within the group (Exhibit 31). Once they have decided on an activity team within their life group, add them to the list of members on that team (Exhibit 33).

Absentees – Life groups can provide valuable assistance to the elders by following up on absent members in their group. The church office can provide the group leaders with a list of members absent from worship each week. A call, card, or e-mail to let absentees know they were missed the previous week will help to alleviate one of the major reasons people leave a congregation or become unfaithful.

Sick & Shut-ins - Benevolent work is one of the major responsibilities of the church and the life groups are an excellent vehicle to help carry out this duty. Depending on the availability of relatives and friends, the sick and shut-ins often need food, transportation and social contact.

Edification & Evangelism – Group leaders should continually observe the spiritual growth of the members in their group and encourage them to accept new and greater responsibilities as they grow. This is how the church develops future leaders in both male and female roles. Most conversions come from friends and relatives of current members. The life/care groups are an excellent source of potential Bible studies with friends and relatives of members. Encourage your members to invite friends and relatives to group social functions.

The key to a successful life group ministry are the people selected as coordinators, group leaders and activity leaders. Effective leaders learn how to delegate responsibility and authority so that the work is accomplished effectively. [See the organizational chart in Exhibit 71]

Fellowship Program

This is a social function that enhances the cohesiveness of a congregation by formalizing the activity of members visiting members and reaching out to visitors. Teams of 10-12 people meet once a month for a meal and fellowship at which time they are also assigned a visit to a member in need or a visitor. At times, visits are assigned simply to get to know other members of the congregation. The teams should be reorganized every six months so that all team members have an opportunity to fellowship with each other over time. The program should be overseen by a mature Christian with good organizational skills. Team leaders should also be dependable members.

Meeting Place – The monthly meetings should be at team members' homes or they can meet at the church building or a restaurant.

Team Members – Couples or singles are welcome. Singles are paired up with another single (male/male or female/female) and visits are made together.

Team Assignments – The fellowship program coordinator assigns team leaders and members and works with the church office in developing visiting lists each month. Announcements are made at the end of each cycle inviting other members to join the fellowship program. Personal invitations can also be made.

Host Responsibility – The monthly host couple plans the menu with simple meals and informs their team members what they should bring. Normally the host prepares the main dish. The male host should prepare a 5 minute devotional to be delivered after dinner and before the business of reviewing last month's visits and assigning the next month's visits. Teams with two females can ask the team leader or another male team member to prepare and deliver the devotional for their meeting.

Meeting Dates – This is a local decision.

Visit Assignments – These include the sick, shut-ins, hospital patients or those that may need encouragement, such as new members. The visits can be made any time during the month in person (preferably) or by a phone call or card. Invitations to lunch or other social events are also an option. Follow-up with visitors should be made the week of the team meeting while the worship experience is still fresh on their minds.

Visit Reports – After the team meal and devotional, the team leader should ask each team member to report on their assigned visit from the last meeting. This report is turned into the program coordinator for record keeping and possible further action by the elders, minister, or church leaders. After reporting, new assignments are made with the host house having first opportunity to choose a visit.

Children – It is recommended that the monthly meetings be adults only. Due to the nature of the meeting small children can be distracting, and if possible, arrangements should be made for babysitting either at home or at the church building by responsible teens.[See the organizational chart in Exhibit 72.]

An effective involvement ministry will help to create a continual sense of ownership by members in the various works of their congregation. Their level of commitment, the quality of their work, and their spirituality will rise as they foster that sense of involvement.

CHAPTER NINE

Bible School
Exodus 18:20

Moses' father-in-law reminded him of his responsibility to teach his people the law and what they must do. Elders have that same responsibility today.

We spend eighteen years, nursery through 12th grade, attempting to educate our children in order to prepare them for the carnal world they will face after completing high school and leaving home. In spite of all that effort, many of them become unfaithful. This is unacceptable to God and should cause every congregational leader to shudder when they read Zechariah 10:2-3 and Hebrews 13:17. We know that parents have primary responsibility for training their children, but the church also has a duty to partner with families in this critical ministry. As the old adage goes, "those that do not learn from history are bound to repeat it." Something went terribly wrong with the training of the Israelite children during Joshua's reign (Judges 2:10). If we are not careful today we will repeat the same mistakes. How can we do an adequate job of training future leaders in the church when we are losing so many of our potential leaders? This trend must stop! Elders and leaders in a congregation must "set the bar high" on the importance of the Bible school ministry. The public and private support and involvement of the leaders is the foundation of a successful ministry.

The challenge before us is to develop an effective, well-rounded and sustainable program to prepare our youth for independent Christian adulthood within the limited resources available to the typical congregation of the Lord's church. Many congregations do not have an Education or Youth minister, but that does not relieve the leaders of the responsibility to train up their youth. The purpose of the next two chapters (Bible School & Youth), is to present some basic principles and practices for a successful training ministry that can be implemented within the resource limits of a typical congregation.

Mission Statement

Before beginning development of a Bible school program, we must answer the obvious question: "What is it we want to accomplish with this ministry?" Development of a mission statement is a good way to focus efforts on your desired goals for this ministry.

Example: "Our Bible school ministry will be an evangelistic and edification based activity that provides students with knowledge of the scriptures sufficient for them to make an informed personal decision to obey the plan of salvation, to faithfully live the Christian life, and grow in the knowledge of our Lord and Savior through the application of Christian principles."

These goals are accomplished by first teaching our children Bible facts, which leads to Bible principles, which leads to the application of these timeless principles to everyday life situations.

Organization

Once a mission statement has been developed, the structure of the Bible school ministry should be determined. Clear lines of authority and responsibility should be established at all levels to ensure the most productive program possible, and to promote continued trust and confidence in the congregation's leaders. Exhibit 34 is a sample organizational chart. This would obviously vary depending on the circumstances at each congregation.

Teachers

Unqualified teachers are often the result of a needs based Bible school ministry that rushes to fill an open slot with the first person willing to step up to the job. As I discussed previously, ministries should be interest/talent-based in order to be successful and sustainable. A quest for new teachers should start with a search in the automated involvement profiles of your members for those adults that have experience in secular and religious teaching and those interested in becoming teachers (Exhibit 30). Those individuals can then be personally contacted (after elder/leader approval), to determine their interest and availability for open teaching positions within the Bible school. They should then be asked to complete the teacher questionnaire to determine their doctrinal positions on a variety of Bible topics (Exhibit 15).

Any "no" answers should be cause for a meeting with church leaders to discuss the acceptability of this person as a teacher. Once approved, the Bible school director, department coordinator or current lead teacher in the prospective class, should review the curriculum and list of students with the new teacher. The mission statement should also be reviewed so that every teacher understands the elders' vision for their Bible school ministry. It is critical that everyone has a "sense of ownership" in this vision. Only then should that person begin their assignment. How long a qualified teacher continues to teach the same class is a matter of judgment. I have seen teachers go on for decades and others rotated every quarter. While these extremes may be appropriate in certain cases, I believe the optimum situation usually lies somewhere in the middle. Students need consistency in their lives and teachers need time to develop skills and familiarity with their students and material.

Training/Evaluation

The Bible school ministry, like the church, is a living organization that will require continual attention in order to maintain its balance. Periodic teacher meetings (quarterly as a minimum) provide an excellent opportunity for leaders at all levels (elder, director, department coordinator) to encourage, inform and train current teachers. Special training by experts in Christian education outside your congregation is available and may be considered as part of the overall training plans each year.

The elders are ultimately responsible for the spiritual food fed to the congregation not only from the pulpit, but in every Bible class (1 Peter 5:2). I recommend that the primary elder over the Bible school and the Bible school director visit classes periodically to observe the teachers and material being taught to evaluate their effectiveness. It should be explained to the students why this person is visiting the class. These visits serve several purposes. They encourage the teachers and students by showing them that the congregational leaders are taking a direct interest in their work. Secondly, they send a message of accountability to the teachers for being on time and prepared for class. Finally, they allow the leaders an opportunity to provide insight into class situations.

Accountability is a great motivator for teachers and students. Leaders should expect their teachers to be in their classrooms when students begin to arrive. If they cannot attend class on a particular day they should notify their co-teacher and/or department coordinator in time to find a replacement or adjust the classes. They should come prepared to teach the assigned lesson. Students should be expected to come to class prepared to participate. They should bring their Bibles, workbooks, and lessons every week. Positive reinforcement in the form of charts or awards is an excellent way to motivate children. Teachers should enlist the help of parents with children who consistently are not prepared for class. Elders should meet with parents of children who do not attend Bible class to determine the reasons and stress the importance of this ministry in their spiritual development.

Curriculum

The same high level of effort that went into developing the mission statement, organization and teachers, must also go into selecting the appropriate curriculum for all classes. Leaders must continually review the material being used and material available for use to ensure classes are accomplishing their purpose according to the mission statement. Waiting until the last week of a quarter to start thinking about the subjects, material and teachers for the next quarter is not an effective way to run a Bible school ministry. Thoughtful long-term planning will result in an effective curriculum taught with appropriate material and taught by teachers who are prepared and enthusiastic about their assignments. Material can be developed locally, purchased from reliable sources or obtained from other congregations. It is not the intent of this chapter to present exhaustive curriculum resources but to lay the ground work for a successful Bible school program, I will discuss below several possible curriculums. Congregational leaders should always be on the lookout for good material when reading church publications, attending various lectureships and meeting with leaders of other congregations.

In addition to the information listed below, I do want to mention several "special" classes that can be extremely useful when taught on a regular basis at every congregation of the Lord's church.

First Principles Class

Preparing our children for Christian adulthood and newly baptized adults for service in the kingdom must start with grounding them in the basic principles of Christianity. Occasionally, long-time members of the church need a refresher course on these subjects as well. I strongly recommend a periodic class on basic Bible doctrine that would cover such subjects as:

1. Books of the Bible
2. Old or New Testament today?
3. What does the Bible say about the church of Christ?
4. Do you worship God acceptably?
5. New Testament music
6. Are you saved?
7. Is man justified by faith and works?
8. Can a saved person fall away?
9. Organization of the church of Christ
10. Qualifications of elders and deacons
11. Where is the soul after death?[12]

Intermediate Class

I attended a first principles class prior to my baptism in 1978 and continued that course of study for a short-time afterward. My next class was a study of the book of Romans and I was completely lost for the entire quarter. It was way over my head. Fortunately, I had strong support from my family or I might have lost interest in Bible study. The purpose of an intermediate or bridge class is to prepare a young Christian for a deeper study of the scriptures in classes with mature Christians. Books such as *Hermeneutics* by D.R. Dungan and *How We Got the Bible* by Neil R. Lightfoot are good material for this class. Frank Chesser's book, *Portrait of God*, which studies the plan of redemption throughout the Bible, would also be an excellent resource as well as Wayne Jackson's *A Study Guide to Greater Bible Knowledge*.

Stewardship

It is common knowledge that many members of the Lord's church do not give as they should. I believe a major reason for this is a lack of understanding about our responsibility to be good stewards of the material blessings God has bestowed upon us. Teaching this subject every other year for at least part of a quarter will provide your members with the information necessary to become and continue to be faithful stewards. Brother V.P. Black has written several books on this subject such as *My God and My Money*.

Personal Evangelism

Very few members of the Lord's church are actively involved in personal Bible studies. Periodic classes with practical lessons on this subject will instill confidence in Christians to reach out to the lost. Material on this subject is plentiful.

Christian Evidences

The secular humanists are bombarding us daily with misinformation about our origins, evolution, the age of the earth, the inspiration of the Bible and many other subjects. Our children and adults need to know the truth. Apologetics Press produces extensive material on these topics.

Sample Curriculums

1. The Cold Harbor Road Church of Christ has developed a very good five year study of the Bible for all classes that is available on CD.[13]

2. Sain Publications offers a six year study of the Old Testament and a six year study of the New Testament. The quarterly topics are shown at Exhibits 35 and 36.[14]

3. Engraving Heavenly Truths offers a four year curriculum for all classes.[15]

4. See Exhibit 37 for a three year rotational curriculum for grades 4 – 12 developed by the Forest Park Church of Christ. A curriculum for grades 1-3 is also available by calling 404-366-3820.

A bulletin board displayed in your foyer area that lists the year's curriculum for all classes will help to maintain interest in Bible study.

This critical ministry deserves the elders' utmost attention. We cannot fail to prepare our children for faithful service in His kingdom. Their souls depend on it.

CHAPTER TEN

Youth
1 Timothy 4:12

Paul taught Timothy that youth should be an example to other believers. Parents and elders have that same responsibility today to teach their youth to become faithful Christians.

As with the Bible school ministry, I recommend starting your planning with development of a mission statement that clearly presents the elders' goals for this work. What do you want to accomplish with your youth program? What resources must be devoted to this effort in order to produce the goals we have established in our mission statement? With or without a full time youth minister, there must be a plan, organizational structure, support from the elders, and devoted resources in order to achieve success in this effort.

Due to the geographic and demographic nature of our lives today, our children often do not live near or go to school with many of their Christian friends from their congregation. They are surrounded by worldly people for much of their week. As parents and church leaders, we must provide opportunities for our children to spend time with other Christians participating in wholesome activities (1 Corinthians 15:33).

Sample Mission Statement

"Encourage spiritual growth, Christian friendships and a servant attitude among our youth during the very challenging teenage years in order to develop strong, faithful Christians who are prepared for the responsibilities of living the adult Christian life."

As noted above, I believe that a good youth program should provide much more than a social outlet for our teens. In order to be successful in helping to prepare our children for adulthood, it should contain activities that promote spiritual maturity, social interaction and a servant attitude. It must also have the continual public support of the eldership and be adequately funded by the congregation's budget. It is essential that the teens believe they are an important part of the congregation. Regardless of whether it is headed up by a full time youth minister, deacon, or mature Christian, the active involvement of the parents and others in the congregation is critical to its success. The youth director should possess motivational, organizational, and leadership skills as well as the ability to relate to the youth.

Sample Organization

> Director/Coordinator
> Team One (Annual Youth Rally)
> Team Two (Evangelism)
> Team Three (Service Projects)
> Team Four (Youth Retreats/Summer Camps)
> Team Five (Social Activities)
> Team Six (Pre-Teens)

In addition to the team leaders, co-leaders and parents, other members should be asked to serve on the teams to support varies events throughout the year. Exhibit 38 contains a sample letter to parents announcing a new youth program. Ministry leadership meetings with the youth director and team leaders should be held on a regular basis to keep the activities on track and everyone motivated. I recommend monthly meetings following reorganization and a minimum of quarterly meetings once the new work is up and running smoothly.

Team Activities

Annual Youth Rally

- Consider holding an annual rally or plan to attend at least one or two area rallies each year. A sample planning outline is shown in Exhibit 39.

Evangelism

- Teach interactive class on how to conduct a personal Bible study.
- Assist with the processing of requests for Bible correspondence courses as part of the congregation's local outreach ministry or in support of foreign evangelism.

- Support promotion of gospel meetings.
- Record boys devotionals for local church sponsored radio program.

Service Projects

- Organize group singing at homes of shut-ins, seniors or nursing homes.
- Assist in the building and grounds clean-up.
- Serve food at congregational meals.
- Perform yard work for shut-ins and widows.
- Volunteer as worship greeters.

Youth Retreats

- Day, weekend trips, and summer camps to promote fellowship and Christian values. A sample medical release form is shown in Exhibit 40. **Any medical form you use should be approved by an attorney or legal counsel.**

Social Activities

- Junior/Senior Banquet (alternative to Prom)
- Amusement parks such as Six Flags
- Bowling
- Movies
- Rafting
- Sporting events
- Aquariums/museums

Pre-Teens

- Parties
- Building/grounds clean-up
- Movies, games, crafts
- Gift baskets for shut-ins

Exhibit 41 is a sample letter to parents.

Budget

Each team leader should submit a proposed budget for the coming year's activities to the youth director. The director should then compile each team's budget into a combined youth ministry budget and submit it to the elders for consideration during the formulation of the congregation's annual budget for the upcoming year.

Promotion

The Youth ministry leaders should always be looking for ways to promote this work.

- Youth activities should be added to the congregation's monthly events calendar.

- A youth ministry link should be added to the church's website.

- A bulletin board should be devoted to youth activities and accomplishments.

- Continual public promotion of youth activities by including them in the announcements each week.

Elders often are not as involved or supportive of the youth program as they are with other more familiar works. They need to recognize this tendency and make an extra effort to provide involved oversight and direction to those working with our youth. See the organizational chart at Exhibit 73.

Lads to Leaders and Leaderettes

I have been involved with Lads to Leaders for over 20 years as a parent, deacon, elder, convention coordinator, and Board member. Now that I am retired, much of my time is devoted to supporting this vital program. As mentioned previously, we are losing many of our children to the world and this travesty must stop! Lads to Leaders & Leaderettes is a leadership training tool that can be tailored to the specific needs of individual congregations as part of their effort to train up children to be strong faithful Christian leaders in their congregations, homes, schools, and communities.

"Leaders do not just happen; they are developed and the sooner the process starts, the better. Where will these people, these leaders come from? Will they just appear someday? The church must deal with these questions and provide a solution." John O. Simmons, MD, elder and member of Lads to Leaders Board of Directors.

"Lads to Leaders has produced more preachers than any other similar program in the Lord's church to my knowledge." *V.P. Black, minister, elder*

"I have been involved in Lads to Leaders from day one. Throughout the years, it has been my privilege to participate. With great joy I have watched it expand and grow. I wish every child in the USA could participate. Every congregation of the Lord's Church, a must." *Charles B. Hodge, minister*

What is the history behind Lads to Leaders & Leaderettes? The elders at the Corder Road Church of Christ in Warner Robins, Georgia asked their minister, Dr. Jack Zorn, in 1968 to train their young men to be leaders in the church and community. In January, 1969, those eight young men gave their first talks at the congregation. From that humble beginning, Lads to Leaders & Leaderettes is now utilized by over 500 congregations with 20,000 people attending one of six National Conventions each spring. Since 1969, over 200,000 young people have been taught effective leadership skills through this program.

How is Lads to Leaders & Leaderettes useful? There are many tools available to assist families and local congregations with spiritual development. Summer camps are good tools but are usually just for one week. Youth rallies and lectureships may only be for a few days. Christian Universities are for those old enough to attend. There is a need for a year-round, Bible-based program that will complement the Bible school curriculum and focus on character building and training our youth to be leaders in all phases of their spiritual and secular lives.

What is the goal of Lads to Leaders & Leaderettes? To provide churches with effective, year-round youth leadership training tools that can be adapted to individual congregational needs.

What is the purpose of Lads to Leaders & Leaderettes? To provide congregations with proven tools to train youth and increase their involvement in the work of the church.

What are the program objectives of Lads to Leaders & Leaderettes? To instill within each student the belief and confidence that he or she can become a positive leader in the home, church, school and community. To instill an appreciation for the contributions of great leaders and the continuing need for righteous leadership. To teach basic leadership principles while providing training and experience to develop leadership skills and effectiveness. To help develop skills which are characteristic of a good leader, such as: study skills, social graces, public speaking, teaching skills, planning skills and organizational skills. To develop attitudes consistent with Christian leadership, such as love for God, people, truth, righteousness, honesty, integrity, and hatred for wickedness, corruption, sin and laziness.

What are the functions of the Lads to Leaders & Leaderettes National Service Center? To develop material, conduct training workshops and hold National Conventions.

What is the National Convention?

This is an opportunity for thousands of young people to gather to recognize the accomplishments of the past year and encourage future growth. Most of the work has already taken place at the home congregation but some events, such as Bible bowl and speech, are held at convention.

Why have a National Convention? It holds our children accountable by establishing a deadline for completing work. It recognizes and encourages the children. Two or more awards are presented to each student on average. It raises the bar in regards to commitment and responsibility. Top-level young speakers and song leaders become role models for others. It is spiritually uplifting. Thousands of boys and girls strive to learn better how to serve Christ.

Who can participate? There are non-competitive events for children from kindergarten to second grade as well as adults. There are, as of this writing, twenty-four non-competitive and eleven competitive events for grades K-12 and adults.[16]

Who can be involved? Anyone and everyone! Lads to Leaders & Leaderettes is not a youth program, it is a congregational program. There is something for everyone to do. Your Lads program would have a group leader who provides overall coordination, teachers for the weekly/monthly classes, event coordinators for such events as speech, song leading and puppets, mentors who encourage individual students, and those who provide transportation to the various events.

What are the foundational principles of Lads to Leaders & Leaderettes?

- A Volunteer Spirit – students lead by stepping out first.

- 100% Cooperation – students lead by learning how to work with others.

- Worthy Goals – students lead by knowing what their purpose is and what steps are necessary to accomplish them.

- Self-Starter – students lead by being internally motivated.

What is the Lads to Leaders & Leaderettes motto? No person will be expected to do tasks without first being provided proper preparation and assistance. This training assures the building of self-esteem and insists that the student accept responsibility for the preparation for a task. Proper preparation produces successful endeavors and repeated successes produce self-esteem. Confident, well-equipped young men and women are leaders.

What is at the heart of Lads to Leaders & Leaderettes? Dr. Zorn has developed and refined ten Leader Pledges over the years that form the core character traits needed by a Christian leader:

1. I am answerable to God and to society (Matthew 22:21).
2. I will overcome pessimism and live a life of faith in God (Philippians 4:13).
3. I am fully responsible for my behavior (Matthew 7:12; Romans 14:12).
4. I am responsible for my agreements and obligations (Matthew 7:12).
5. I pursue honest work to meet my responsibilities (1 Timothy 5:8).
6. I honor and obey my parents and respect persons in authority (Ephesians 6:2).
7. I respect my body as the creation of God and use it for His glory (1 Corinthians 6:20).
8. I choose for my friends those who enjoy doing good (1 Corinthians 15:33).
9. I lead in building character and in demonstrating integrity (Philippians 2:22).
10. I lead in second-mile service to others (Matthew 5:41).

What training material is available?

1. Teacher/Student Manuals
2. Junior Leader (grades K-5)
3. PEARLS Study Series (various Bible book studies)
4. Gifts (Girls in Fellowship and Team Study) grades 6-12
5. Guard (Guys Understanding Authority and Real Discipleship) grades 6-12

6. Headed to the Office (teen boys study on preparing for church leadership), grades 6-12

7. Training Five-Talent Servants Handbook

8. Bible Bowl Questions

9. Rules Book (download from website)

Information regarding college scholarships, how to start a Lads program at your congregation and contact information is shown in Exhibit 42.

Conclusion

These are perilous times for the Lord's church. Satan is attacking our youth at every opportunity. We are losing many of our children to the world. We teach them sports and take them to recreational and social activities. However, unless we do more teaching and less entertaining, we will leave them unprepared to face a secular world filled with material and sensual enticements. They will be puzzled about their beliefs, easily pulled away from the truth and easy targets for false teachers. Congregations have reported that over 90% of their children that participated in the Lads to Leaders & Leaderettes Program have remained faithful well into their adult lives.

"And you shall teach them the statues and the laws and show them the way in which they must walk and the work they must do (Exodus 18:20). Moses provided wise counsel to the parents of his generation and his words are timeless.

May our prayer from today forward be that the day will come when we will no longer have to pray to God for forgiveness for what we have failed to do in preparing our youth for service in His kingdom.

CHAPTER ELEVEN

Elder/Preacher Relations
2 Timothy 4:2

Paul charged Timothy to preach the Word. Elders should provide similar direction to their preacher.

Elders and preachers share a unique relationship within a congregation. We know that elders are ultimately responsible to God for their effectiveness in leading the congregation (Hebrews 13:17). Preachers are accountable to God on the one hand, but also labor under the oversight of the elders as members of their congregation. In one sense they work *with* the elders as part of the leadership team and in another sense work *for* the elders as an employee of the congregation. The dual nature of this relationship presents challenges and potential difficulties if not handled properly. I have talked with preachers who complain that their elders are disengaged and lack the initiative to pro-actively lead their congregations and provide leadership, direction, and support for the preacher's efforts. No doubt this is frustrating to preachers and often leads to them taking on a role as de facto pastor of their flock. I have also talked with elders who complain that their preachers are unwilling to take direction from them and do not devote sufficient effort in accomplishing their responsibilities. It is not my intention in this chapter to take sides on this complicated relationship, but to provide information on possible ways to structure the relationship to maximize the effectiveness of the leadership team.

Hiring a Preacher

This is obviously one of the most important and far reaching decisions that elders will make and should never be taken lightly. Intensive research and investigation is required to ensure the best choice is made. Although word-of-mouth will generate potential candidates, elders should take a pro-active stance and contact other elders, preachers, friends, or preaching schools for leads. Men that have expressed interest in the position or have been recommended by a reliable source should be investigated to determine if an unannounced visit to their congregation's services to hear them preach is worthwhile. Visiting a congregation to hear a "typical" sermon preached by the prospective candidate will often reveal more than the CD/DVD he provides upon request. A telephone call can then be made to discuss the candidate's interest, solicit a resume` and request the completion of a preacher questionnaire. A sample can be found at Exhibit 15. This may be followed with an invitation to speak to the congregation, meet with the elders and visit the area in which the potential preacher and his family may be working. The elders' preparation for this initial meeting is very important. An agenda should be developed that includes specific questions on a variety of subjects as listed on the Potential Preacher Evaluation Form (Exhibit 43). In "Recognizing Wolves at the Door," Aubrey Johnson suggests a useful set of questions to ask when interviewing a potential preacher in order to eliminate ambiguous responses that might veil doctrinal problems:[17]

1. *Baptism*—Do you believe there are times today when God forgives sin before or apart from baptism (immersion)?

2. *Fellowship*—Do you believe some unbaptized believers should be recognized as Christians?

3. *Worship*—Does it violate Scripture to worship God in song with the accompaniment of a piano if it does not create division? Does the Bible limit partaking of the Lord's Supper to the first day of the week?

4. *Women's Roles*—Is it a violation of Scripture for women to lead songs or prayers in public settings where Christian men are present?

5. *Elders' Authority*—Do elders have positional authority to direct the affairs of the local church, or does the Bible limit their influence to moral authority?

6. *Bible Authority*—Is the Bible inerrant (free of factual discrepancies) and the final authority in deciding all matters of religious faith and practice (the work, manner of worship, organization, terms of admission, name and morals of the church)?

7. *Bible Interpretation*—Do you consider the "argument from silence" a beneficial method of biblical interpretation or a flawed and divisive one?

8. *Unity*—Do you support unity and closer fellowship with Christian churches that remain committed to using instrumental music in worship?

Also, the duties and responsibilities for this position should be discussed in detail (Exhibits 44 & 45). After the initial meeting, each elder should independently complete Exhibit 43 and then the totals should be averaged to determine a score for each applicant. This numerical evaluation would be used along with observations and other intangibles to determine if the individual is a legitimate candidate. If both parties are agreeable, a second meeting should be held to discuss economic details such as salary, benefits, moving expenses, and housing.

Signing a formal contract is a local decision, but I would recommend, as a minimum, that both parties sign an agreement that states the elders or preacher will provide the other party a minimum of ninety days' notice of termination of employment. The potential preacher should agree that the elders have the right to terminate his employment for doctrinal or discretionary reasons. If at some point in the future, the elders determine it is time for a change in preachers, I would strongly recommend that they provide the ninety days severance pay immediately and terminate employment. Allowing him to continue to preach and work for the congregation during this ninety day period is rarely a pleasant or productive experience.

Evaluating a Preacher

The amount and nature of the oversight of a preacher will vary depending on the relationship at each congregation. In some situations, elders rarely meet with their preacher and provide little, if any, direction or oversight. In other situations, elders have been known to micromanage him to the point that he is accountable for every minute of his day. Reasonable oversight lies somewhere between these two extremes. At a minimum, both parties should have a clear understanding of what the elders expect from the preacher. It is rare that an elder will be at the church building all day or even every day of the week. Preachers, by the nature of their responsibilities, work independently much of the time. The extent of that independence should be determined by how well he is carrying out his assigned duties. At a minimum, it is suggested that he complete a weekly activity report (Exhibit 44). These should be reviewed by each elder, utilized during regular staff meetings and filed for use during his annual evaluation.

As previously mentioned, the duties and responsibilities of the preacher should be specifically listed in writing so as to minimize any misunderstandings about what the elders expect. Exhibit 44 is a sample that lists duties, responsibilities, expectations, objectives, reviews, and ratings. The level of detail can be adjusted based on the circumstances at local congregations, but keep in mind that failing to define the responsibilities of a local preacher can lead to confusion in expectations.

Your preacher is obviously a critical part of the leadership team and should be included in many planning and oversight decisions made by the elders. His wise counsel is extremely valuable.

That being said, elders must always remember that the Holy Scriptures clearly state that they are the ones ultimately accountable to God for the welfare of their congregation. (Hebrews 13:17).

CHAPTER TWELVE

Gospel Meetings/Seminars/Lectures
Ephesians 4:11-13

Paul stresses the importance of evangelizing, equipping, and edifying the body of Christ. There are various activities that can support these goals.

Congregations invest significant resources each year in planning and implementing various activities to edify their members and reach their communities with the truth from God's Word. As good stewards of the Lord's possessions, it is the elders' responsibility to ensure that these efforts are accomplished in the most productive manner possible.

Scheduling

Potential speakers should be contacted one to three years in advance (especially the popular ones) to establish tentative dates and topics. It is understood that changing circumstances may dictate adjustments to the schedule. The individual(s) involved in this ministry should continue planning events each year to maintain a rolling schedule one to three years ahead (Exhibit 46).

Once a verbal agreement has been reached with a speaker, a letter should be sent along with the speaker questionnaire to confirm the meeting (Exhibits 47 & 15). A suspense date should be set up to ensure a timely return of the questionnaire. "No" answers to any of the questions should be dealt with immediately upon receipt of the questionnaire. Unresolved issues may necessitate a withdrawal of the invitation to speak. A gospel meeting checklist should be used to track the preparation for each meeting to ensure all actions are completed at the proper time (Exhibit 48).

The general purpose of the meeting and possible topics should be discussed with the speaker during the initial verbal contact. Additional specific information on topics and scheduling should be provided well in advance of the meeting dates. The speaker should be notified of any changes or cancellation of the scheduled meeting. If, for any reason the speaker is no longer desired an explanation should be provided.

Transportation

If the speaker chooses to drive his personal vehicle, reimbursement could be determined by using the current federal government mileage rate for the round trip and vicinity miles traveled.[18] If the distance necessitates more than one day's drive, the speaker would be expected to fly or drive and cover the in-route lodging and meal expenses himself. Exceptions to this policy would be on a case-by-case basis.

If the speaker flies, he should purchase the most economical coach class ticket possible. Arrangements should be made to meet him upon his arrival at the airport and provide local transportation.

Lodging /Meals

Thirty days prior to the meeting, the speaker should be contacted to confirm his lodging preference (hotel, church owned house, member's house). The name, address, and phone number of the lodging facility should be provided to the speaker as early as possible.

Meal plans should take into account any dietary restrictions, the timing of dinners (before/after speaking), and scheduling meals with members.

Finances

After receipt and review of the speaker questionnaire, the cover letter and itemized travel expense record should be sent to the speaker (Exhibits 49 & 50). The letter informs him of the proposed payment for his services. The exception would be for speakers that have established fees. This letter should be sent no later than three months prior to the meeting date.

Speakers should be treated the same as any professional person that provides services to the congregation in regards to compensation for services provided. What other professional would provide service without knowing the rate or amount of compensation before commencing the work?

A separate check should be provided for travel expenses associated with mileage, meals, airfare, ground transportation, and airport parking. Exhibit 49 should be completed by the speaker and submitted to the elders for reimbursement before the meeting ends. The two checks (expense & speaking fee) should be given to the speaker prior to the last day of the meeting so that he may cash them locally, if desired.

Onsite Activities

Your preacher or one of the elders would normally be responsible for coordinating with the speaker on his daily activities during the meeting. Activities could include meals with members, visits, and Bible studies.

Promotion

Various avenues are available to promote your upcoming meeting within the community. If you use House-to-House or a similar locally produced publication, the meeting should be advertised 30-60 days in advance in your mail out. Post cards, billboards, radio, television, web site, newspapers, and your building sign are options as well.

After Meeting Review

A file folder should be created for each meeting to maintain relevant material (letters, questionnaire, forms). Comments, observations and recommendations should be collected within two weeks after the meeting and filed for future use (Exhibit 51).

Special meetings, if planned and executed properly, can be an effective tool in edifying the congregation and reaching out to the lost in your local communities.

CHAPTER THIRTEEN

Finances
Titus 1:7

One of the qualifications of an elder is to be wise and prudent with the stewardship of the financial resources entrusted to them.

One of the quickest ways for elders to lose the trust and confidence of their congregation is to mishandle the contributions or even give the appearance of mishandling them. Every care must be taken to ensure that the Lord's monetary resources are utilized in accordance with the highest ethical, moral, legal, and scriptural standards. Certain duties and responsibilities can be delegated to the deacons, the preacher or other responsible persons, but the elders must stay connected to all activities within their congregation, especially those involving money (Nahum 3:18).

The larger the congregation, the more employees it will generally have and the more assets and activities it will have to manage. The systems in place to develop a budget, manage employee pay and withholdings, and process payments for products and services will vary depending on the size and complexity of the congregation.

As with much of the information in this book, the suggestions below are geared toward an average size congregation of the Lord's church with about 100 members, which can benefit from practical information about the various aspects of overseeing contributions. The processes and documents discussed below are certainly not the only effective method to accomplish this critical responsibility.

Budget

The financial process starts each year with the development of a congregation's budget. Assuming your fiscal year is also the calendar year, the deacons and ministry directors should be asked to submit their itemized budget proposals to the elders by October in order to provide them ample time to complete the budget development process before the start of the new year (Exhibit 52). The various activities and material that make up that final figure should be listed. Once all ministry budget proposals are received, the elders and possibly other responsible persons would then meet to formulate the congregation's proposed budget for the following year. This draft would then be presented to the deacons for their review, questions, and input.

The elders should then present the proposed budget to the congregation by the beginning of December for their review and input (Exhibits 53 & 54). This can be done during a Bible class hour attended by all adults and possibly the senior high school children. All elders should participate in this presentation in which each budget item is explained. Allow some time at the end for a question and answer session.

One week should be given for members to submit questions and comments or meet with the elders on any budget issues prior to finalizing the next year's budget. The following Sunday purpose sheets could be distributed to the adults while an elder explains again the reason for obtaining this information (Exhibits 55 & 53). This is not a binding contract, but merely information to assist the elders in developing a workable budget based on reasonable expectations of weekly contributions from the members.

Contributions

After services, the collected funds should be counted, in private, by at least two responsible members, a tabulation sheet signed and dated by both parties and the funds secured until the deposit is made on Monday. Weekly and monthly contributions should be tracked against the budget (Exhibits 56 & 57). A monthly budget should also be prepared that provides data on last year's total expenditures, this year's annual budget and the by-item expenditures as of the end of each month in order to provide the elders with current information to manage the day-to-day activities of the congregation (Exhibit 58). Adjustments may have to be made if contributions are continually running below the budgeted amounts each week.

Accounts

Weekly contributions could be deposited into a general checking account each Monday from which routine bills, payroll, and other daily expenses can be paid. Transfers from this account to a special or escrow checking account could be made monthly in order to ensure funds were available for periodic expenses such as gospel meetings, benevolence, vehicle repair/purchase, and insurance. See Exhibit 59 for a sample activity record for this account.

Checks

Reimbursement checks should be issued after the completion of a check request form that identifies the purpose and recipient of the check, and the ministry or item code to which the amount will be charged (Exhibit 60). These forms should be approved by an elder or responsible individual, prior to the check being issued by the member or members (dual signatures) assigned that duty.

Public Accountant

Use of an outside accounting firm to handle various bookkeeping and employee reporting requirements is a local decision. If there are no hourly or salaried employees (preacher, secretary or janitor can be paid as independent contractors) this expense may not be justified. If there are employees subject to withholding of various taxes, 401k and matching contributions, it may be prudent to enlist the services of a qualified third party accountant. If you hire a CPA, the weekly deposit amount, along with any bills to be paid, can be e-mailed to the CPA on Monday or Tuesday. The CPA can then prepare the invoice and payroll checks for signature and overnight them to the church for processing by Thursday. The CPA should maintain records for employee withholding and regulatory filings.

It is a simple fact of life that little can be accomplished in a congregation without adequate funding and wise use of those funds. Elders should be directly involved in this critical area.

CHAPTER FOURTEEN

Daily Administration
1 Corinthians 14:40

Paul reminds us of the importance of order in the Lord's church. This does not happen by accident. It must be planned and executed in all phases of the work.

This last chapter will cover various administrative topics that do not fall directly under one of the previously discussed ministries. As I have mentioned in earlier chapters, the ability of the elders to effectively lead their congregation rests primarily on the trust and respect they earn from the congregation. Consistent and reasonable policies on routine day-to-day activities within the church will enhance the reputation of an eldership as being wise and sober minded.

Nomination/Installation of elders

Chapter Two discussed the need to develop leaders. When it comes time to nominate and install new elders, it is important that the process be accomplished in the appropriate manner. Exhibits 61 & 62 provide sample procedures for these functions to include handling allegations from members that a nominated man is not scripturally qualified to be an elder. Allegations should be in writing, specific, and signed by a member. Elders should then promptly, thoroughly, and discreetly investigate the charges to include, if appropriate, meeting with the nominee and the member to clear up, if possible, any misunderstandings or misconceptions about the allegations. Keep in mind that although personality conflicts are not uncommon among members of a congregation they are not, in and of themselves, a valid reason for disqualifying someone from becoming an elder. Once a decision is made, the elders must stand firm. If they decide to proceed with installing the new elder, no public explanation is necessary other than the statement contained in Exhibit 62 that no scriptural reason was found to disqualify the nominee. If they decide to withdraw the nomination, then a simple public statement should be made by the elders without detailing the reasons for the withdrawal.

Liability Insurance

I strongly recommend that the elders and preachers be protected against law suits by members, former members, or those outside the church. This type of liability insurance is relatively inexpensive and will bring peace of mind to local leaders as they deal with important and often sensitive issues involving their congregation.

Eldership Meetings

I know of elderships at the opposite ends of the meeting spectrum. Some elders constantly meet behind closed doors and are rarely seen among their congregations, while others meet so rarely that the preacher must hunt them down to get a consensus on pending action. As usual, somewhere between those two extremes is most logical. I have found that weekly meetings, either Sunday or a week night, are the most effective at handling the congregation's business in a timely and effective manner. Elders should rotate the chairmanship (one to three months) of these meetings and have an established agenda. It is a good idea to start each meeting with a prayer. Discuss delinquents and local outreach efforts before bringing up more routine matters such as old business, mail received since the last meeting, ministry reports from each elder, and new business. Including the preacher in these routine meetings is a local decision, but I would recommend he attend in most cases since he is an integral part of the leadership of a congregation. The meeting would then be closed with a prayer.

Rotation of Assignments

Certain ministry work, such as delinquents, is often more difficult and demanding than others. Consideration should be given to rotating elder assignments on an annual basis to lessen the possibility of burn out or one elder becoming entrenched in a particular work. This also ensures that every elder has firsthand experience in directly overseeing each ministry. It is recommended that each ministry be overseen by a primary elder who then reports to the eldership on this work. This will increase the effectiveness of each ministry by establishing clear lines of communication between each deacon or ministry leader and the eldership. Routine decisions can be made by the ministry leader and more complex situations discussed with the primary elder who keeps the eldership informed of activities within his ministries.

Elder Retreats

As I discussed earlier, leaders should not only deal with the routine responsibilities of leading their congregation, but should also be men of vision. Often elders get bogged down in dealing with mundane issues throughout the year and fail to take time to plan for the long term welfare of the congregation as well as reenergizing their minds and hearts for the challenges that lie ahead. This can be done at an annual retreat preferably away from the building and even out of the local area. The preacher and deacons may be included for all or part of the retreat depending on the proposed agenda. Wives may also be included, but be careful not to give the impression this is holiday getaway at the church's expense. A formal agenda should be prepared to ensure a productive meeting with minutes being recorded so that follow up assignments can be tracked and decisions noted. Suggested agenda items may include: new elders and deacons, missionary work, growth opportunities, capital improvements, finances, new Bible school classes, attendance and contribution trends, ministry reviews, inactive members, youth, gospel meetings, benevolence, and member contributions.

Elder Visibility

Shepherds are always recognized by their sheep because they spend time among them. They do not lead their flocks from inside the farm house but work in the fields among them. Elders should take every opportunity to be seen and heard by the congregation. Leaving these opportunities to the preacher can perpetuate the impression that he is fulfilling a pastoral role. Elders should be one of the first to arrive at the building on Sundays and Wednesdays and one of the last to leave. Mingle with the members before and after services. I also recommend that an elder make opening announcements, stand up front during the invitation song, and lead prayer for those who respond. These activities send a strong public message that the elders truly are shepherds of their flock. It is not necessary that all elders attend every ministry activity or social event involving members of the congregation but it is wise to have one elder attend these functions, preferably the one with direct oversight of that ministry. The subtle message sent by this visibility shows that the leaders are concerned about all the work and the members of the congregation.

Visiting

This is a necessary and sometimes difficult function of the eldership. Members often live in widely dispersed areas and lead very busy lives. Scheduling a time to visit is not always easy, but elders should get into the homes of the congregation on a regular basis to establish the personal relationships necessary to protect and nurture them. The fact that elders take the time to make a personal visit will make a lasting impression on most members. In order to ensure that all members are visited by at least one elder, maintain a system to assign visits during the weekly meetings with each elder reporting on their visit at the next week's meeting. Elders should not visit alone in most cases, especially with single women. His wife, another elder, deacon or the preacher should accompany him on visits.

Note Cards

It is often a nice gesture to send hand written notes of encouragement to members. The message can be a simple thanks for a job well done or appreciation for the influence that person projected on those around them.

Stewardship

This subject almost deserves a chapter of its own. I will preface this discussion with a simple but often overlooked fact. Christians can lose their souls because of their attitude and actions in regard to their giving. Elders should make every effort to see that this does not happen to anyone under their oversight (Hebrews 13:17).

It is common knowledge that some members often don't give as they should. This places their souls in danger of being lost. Although there are cultural and economic differences among congregations, a good gauge of giving is the average "per person in attendance" amount contributed each week. (Example: 150 people in attendance divided by a total contribution of $3,000 would result in an average per person contribution of $20) Why do some groups with similar financial circumstances give significantly different average amounts each week? I believe, in most cases, there are specific reasons for these variations as discussed in the following paragraphs. Elders must get past this notion that talking to people about their giving is somehow "meddling". Will the Lord accept this excuse on judgment day when he asks elders why, when they knew one of their members was not giving as they should, they failed to address this soul threatening situation?

What can be done to improve the corporate and personal giving in a congregation? In addition to the classes on stewardship previously discussed, the following suggestions should prove useful:

Sermons – Ask your preacher to bring at least two lessons a year on various aspects of stewardship.

Announcements – If contributions are trending down, and the congregation is under budget, members should be informed and motivated to improve their giving. Special one-time giving over the weekly contribution can be effective in making up a shortfall at any time during the year. A series of announcements, well ahead of the special contribution Sunday, will energize the members and give them time to plan their part in this activity.

Finances – People will be more inclined to give if they believe that their money is being used wisely. Elders should keep the congregation informed of their efforts to be good stewards of the members' contributions.

Review – This suggestion is bound to raise some eyebrows but, it can be effective at improving personal stewardship, if handled properly. Elders should review the annual contribution of all members and identify those whose amounts or inconsistencies that would merit further investigation. Only those with obvious or unexplained issues such as no contribution for an extended period or very minimal contributions should be addressed. Two elders would schedule a meeting with each person or couple to discuss this issue, preferably without divulging the purpose of the meeting in advance. The key to the success of these meetings is the thoughtful manner in which they are conducted.

A discussion outline that has proven consistently successful in dealing with this sensitive subject is shown in Exhibit 63.

Prospective Members

When a person or family indicates they are interested in placing membership, I recommend they be given information to review prior to meeting with the elders (Exhibit 64). This will help to prepare them for the discussion and answer some of their questions. Once the meeting is scheduled, a checklist can be used to ensure all points are covered (Exhibit 65). After all issues and questions have been discussed to everyone's satisfaction, the person or family would then place membership. General information should be obtained by completing the new member information request in addition to filling out the involvement profile discussed in an earlier chapter (Exhibit 66).

Office Staff

Clear lines of authority should exist with all staff personnel such as the secretary and maintenance people. They should have written job descriptions that clearly state their duties and to whom they report for supervision.

Annual Ministry Rating

The elders or leaders should individually rate each ministry in the congregation once a year on the strength and effectiveness of its work. A listing of all ministries should be given to each person who would then indicate their evaluation by placing an "S" (strong), "W" (weak) or "N" (neutral) beside each item. As part of the planning for the coming year, these assessments should be compared and discussed. Plans to strengthen those ministries with a consensus rating of "weak" should be a priority.

State of the Congregation

Each January, the elders could set aside time to publicly review the events and accomplishments of the congregation during the past year and present the planned events/actions for the coming year. The purpose of this address is to energize the members by reviewing the work done last year and promoting the events for the coming year. As discussed earlier, this helps to create a "sense of ownership" in the work of the congregation with individual members. The topics you discuss might include appointment of elders/deacons, gospel meetings, seminars, new classes, youth events, VBS, benevolent efforts, and campaigns.

Planning Forum

The purpose of a planning forum is to tap into a wealth of ideas generated by members of the congregation for the work of the church for the upcoming year. These meetings can be held in manageable groups, such as your life groups, in the early fall of each year. Prior to these meetings, a cover letter and planning questionnaire could be sent to all members (Exhibits 67 & 68). This is an excellent way to reinforce member involvement in the work of the congregation.

Benevolence

This ministry deserves the elders' strong support and oversight since it is a very important work of the church the two keys to an effective benevolence program are selecting the right person to direct this work and having effective systems in place to ensure deserving people are served in a timely and prudent manner. A mature person with the experience in dealing with sensitive situations is a must for this ministry. He must have wisdom and compassion and yet be insightful enough to spot those people who are not truly in need but simply trying to work area organizations for money. The ministry director must work within the budget set for benevolence and within the monetary limits set by the elders for situations involving members and non-members. The extent of his access to church funds is a local decision. Clear guidelines should be established by the elders so that the benevolence ministry director can effectively carry out his responsibilities.

- *Non-Members* – Benevolent requests from non-members generally come in by phone although some may come to the building in person. A record should be made of their names, addresses, and phone numbers for possible evangelistic follow up and to ensure they are not taking undue advantage of your generosity. I do not recommend giving money directly to non-members, but that is a local decision. Requests for gasoline can be satisfied by following the person to the nearest station and filling up their vehicle by church or personal credit card. Requests for help with rent or utilities can be taken care of by paying the landlord or company directly thus eliminating the possibility of someone using these requests as a way to obtain cash for other purposes. Requests for food can be filled from the church pantry or by use of gift certificates at a local grocery store. These certificates are numbered, have the church name on them and cannot be used for alcohol or tobacco or returned to the store for cash. They come in various denominations. The use of these certificates eliminates the problems that come with storing perishable food stuffs at the church building. Delivery of food or certificates should never be handled alone nor do I recommend entering a stranger's house or apartment. They should come to the car to pick up the assistance if they cannot come to the building.

- *Members* – Benevolent requests from members should be referred to the elders so that they are aware of the physical needs of these people. The extent of help is an elders' decision along with input from the ministry director.

Policies

Inconsistent application of policies on routine activities will be a source of agitation to members and will eventually erode their trust and confidence in the eldership's ability to lead the congregation. Developing reasonable policies and applying them in a consistent manner, will strengthen the leadership and help maintain harmony among the members. These administrative policies should be in writing and available to the congregation. Exhibit 69 contains sample policies on weddings, funerals, baby and wedding showers, flowers, conducting business on church property, use of the fellowship hall, loaning tables and chairs, use of vans/buses, office equipment, and church owned houses.

Security

It is an unfortunate fact of life today that crime is everywhere. No longer can rural congregations leave their building open without fear of unauthorized entry. In order to protect the building and its contents as well as the staff and members, a sound policy on security should be established and followed. Access to the facilities should be controlled by prudent use of locks with consideration given to more advanced equipment such as alarms, cameras, and lighting if the area or situation dictates. Leaders must err on the side of caution when it comes to the security of the people worshipping and working at the building. Consideration should be given to a "step up" key system that allows access to various areas of the building(s) based on need to enter. All keys would open the outside doors, but access to inner rooms would be restricted to people with a need to enter those places. Each person would still have only one key but that key would open different doors depending on their authorized access. Keys should be numbered and a log maintained. Members should sign for the keys assigned to them.

Seniors Ministry

As the baby boomer generation ages, this age group will continue to grow in almost every congregation. There is a wealth of knowledge, experience, and, contrary to belief, energy in our seniors and they deserve the support and involvement of the elders. I recommend a deacon be appointed over this vital ministry and a portion of the congregation's budget be set aside to support the activities of seniors. The activities should include more than just field trips and other social functions. This group can and will contribute to the success of other ministries such as youth, local outreach, and benevolence.

Door Hangers

I mentioned these earlier when discussing visits to members. They can be made at the church building and serve a variety of purposes when visiting sick/shut-ins, delinquents, visitors, or members. A simple preprinted statement with lines for personal comments will provide an easy way to let people know that someone cared enough to make a personal visit. These can be color coded to identify the type of visit.

Building/Property Signs

It is very annoying to see a commercial sign that is in need of repair or missing letters or lighting. That company is sending the worse possible message to everyone who sees their sign. The message is, "We don't care enough about our business, product or service to maintain our advertising." The same can be said about signs identifying our congregations. As we all know, we only have one opportunity to make a good first impression and our signs are often the first thing a visitor sees when approaching our building. Special attention should be given to maintaining attractive and effective signage.

Transportation

The condition of your vans and buses are a safety, morale and outreach issue. How devastating would it be to have an accident with injuries or death because a church vehicle was not properly maintained? What message are you sending to the members, visitors and general public with the condition of your congregation's vehicles? Make sure all drivers have the appropriate licenses and approval of your insurance carrier. I would recommend a responsible deacon or mature Christian be assigned to oversee transportation and adequate funding be made available to maintain all vehicles.

Identifying of elders, deacons and preachers

Consideration should be given to these individuals wearing some type of name tag or badge during services, as well as posting pictures in your foyer area with their names and titles. Deacons' pictures should also have their ministry assignments and phone numbers listed. This information will be especially helpful to visitors and new members. Your directory should identify the elders, deacons and preachers and their assigned ministries.

The items in this chapter may seem incidental at first glance, but they contribute to the overall effectiveness of the elders' work of leading their congregation by improving the level of trust and confidence the congregation has in their leadership.

Conclusion
Ecclesiastes 12:13,14

Solomon in all his wisdom, finally at the end of his life, realized that all of man's duty to God came down to showing Him reverence (Godly fear) and keeping His commandments. Those children in the Kingdom that have been given more talent will be expected to produce greater outcomes and their deeds (or lack of them) will be brought forth on judgment day. Elderships have been given a small piece of His kingdom to oversee and God requires them to apply the principles found in His Word, the Bible, to effectively carry out the mission that Christ invoked during His earthly ministry: "Seek and save the lost."

It is my hope and prayer that the information contained in this book will provide worthwhile guidance to those men who have chosen to stand in the gap.

God Bless,

Jim Whitmire

1. George Santayana, *"Reason and Common Sense"*

2. Russ Burcham *"Something Better,"* Gospel Advocate 151.2 (February 2009):23.

3. Matthew Henry, *Matthew Henry's Commentary: Acts to Romans,* vol. 6 (Peabody, MA: Hendrickson, 1991), 656.

4. John Gardner, *"Leaders and Followers,"* Liberal Education 73 (1987):4-8.

5. Don Campbell, *"Leaders Must Follow the Shepherd,"* Gospel Advocate 151.2 (February 2009): 17-19.

6. John Wooden, *Wooden on Leadership: How to Create a Winning Organization* (New York: McGraw-Hill, 2005), 30.

7. For more information on the concept of upward delegation see William Oncken, Jr., Donald L. Wass, and Stephen R. Covey, *"Management Time: Who's Got the Monkey,"* Harvard Business Review 77.6 (1999): 178-186.

8. Kenneth Blanchard and Spencer Johnson, *"The One Minute Manager"* (New York: William George Morrow and Company, 1982): 61.

9. Bobby Bates' *Back to the Bible,* Jerry Jenkins' *God Speaks Today,* Robert Martin's *Pacific Islands Bible School Soul Winning Studies,* Steve Vice's *God's Word the Bible and Salvation,* forestparkchurch@yahoo.com.

10. For more information visit www.fishersofmen.net

11. For more information contact Gary Bodine at the Borger Church of Christ, P.O. Box 3364, Borger, Texas 79008. Phone number 806-274-6354.

12. These lessons can be developed locally or obtained from Forest Park Church of Christ at 404-366-3820 or by e-mailing forestparkchurch@yahoo.com. Other resources include the following: *The beginning of Our Confidence* by David Pharr; *Things Surely Believed Among Us* by Paul Rodgers; and *Now That I Am in Christ* by Jim Massey.

13. Contact Cold Harbor Church of Christ at 804-746-8224 or e-mail office@cold-harbor-road.org

14. For orders call 615-363-6905 or e-mail psain@bellsouth.net

15. For more information see www.heavenlytruths.com

16. Review the Rules book at the Lads website www.lads-to-leaders.org for an explanation of each event.

17. Aubrey Johnson, *"Recognizing Wolves at the Door,"* Gospel Advocate 151.10 (October, 2009): 36.

18. This rate can be found at www.gsa.gov then click on "POV Mileage Reimbursement" on the left side of the page.

Exhibits

1. Prospective elder/deacon matrix

2. List of books and periodicals for prospective/current elders/deacons

3. Attendance spreadsheet

4. First disciplinary letter

5. Second disciplinary letter

6. Third disciplinary letter

7. Statement placing delinquent member's name before the congregation

8. Statement withdrawing congregational fellowship with delinquent member

9. Fourth disciplinary letter – withdrawal of fellowship

10. Fifth disciplinary letter – follow up to disfellowship

11. Follow up letter to congregation on disfellowhshipped member

12. Lesson on church discipline

13. Prospective deacons Class

14. Prospective deacon discussion outline

15. Questionnaire

16. Deacon commitment questionnaire

17. Deacon nomination procedures

18. Deacon installation procedures

19. Elder/Deacon assignments

20. Deacon ministry descriptions

21. Guidelines for widows and the elderly

22. Annual deacons retreat agenda

23. Terms of oversight agreement – missionaries

24. Packing list

25. Preparation outline for short term missionary campaigns

26. Visitors report

27. Visitors follow-up report

28. Community Involvement report

29. New members' orientation class outline

30. Involvement profile

31. Life group committees and chairperson(s)

32. Life group member profile

33. Life group activity list

34. Bible school organizational chart

35. Sain Old Testament curriculum

36. Sain New Testament curriculum

37. Forest Park 4th-12th grade curriculum

38. Letter to parents about youth ministry

39. Youth rally planning outline

40. Medical release form

41. Letter to parents about pre-teen program

42. Lads to Leaders information

43. Preacher evaluation form

44. Preacher duties/responsibilities

45. Preacher weekly activity report

46. Gospel meeting schedule

47. Gospel meeting initial letter to speaker

48. Gospel meeting checklist

49. Gospel meeting cover letter

50. Gospel meeting itemized travel expense record

51. Gospel meeting evaluation form

52. Ministry budget proposal

53. Elders budget presentation

54. Budget proposal

55. Purpose sheet

56. Monthly contributions

57. Monthly contribution report

58. Interim budget

59. Special/escrow account report

60. Check request

61. Elder nomination

62. Elder installation

63. Stewardship discussion outline

64. Prospective members package

65. Prospective member interview checklist

66. New member information request

67. Planning meeting cover letter

68. Planning meeting questionnaire

69. Sample policies

70. Local outreach organizational chart

71. Life group organizational chart

72. Fellowship program organizational chart

73. Youth program organizational chart

Exhibit 1

Developing Future Leaders

AT THE _____

Church of Christ

I.   Identify men in the congregation that display the desire and potential for leadership

II.   Assign each man a leadership potential rating (LPR) consisting of a timeframe/position code. The numbers 1-3, 3-5, 5+,representing years and D and E representing deacon and elder. The codes are as follows: (1-3/D), (3-5/D), (5+D), (1-3/E), (3-5/E), (5+/E)

III. Note each man's current assignment(s)

IV.   Assign an elder to mentor each man

V.   Elders develop possible future leadership assignments/training for each man

VI.   Elder (mentor) meet with each assigned man/wife to discuss his desire for leadership and future assignments/training

VII. Elders review and revise if appropriate each man's progress and LPR during the elders' annual retreat

VIII. Elder (mentor) meets annually with each man/wife to review last year's progress and plan training and assignments for the coming year

Name	Elder	Current Assignment	LPR
John Smith	Doe	Deacon – youth	3-5/E
Tim Jones	Lane	Transportation	1-3/D
Jim Barnes	Howard	Finances	E-Now
Bob Vice	Doe	Prison ministry	D-Now

Exhibit 2

Recommended Publications

Surprising Insights from the Unchurched – Thom S. Rainer

Encouraging Deacons – Thomas Holland

360 degree Leader – John Maxwell

Shepherds, Ancient Training for Modern Shepherds – J.J. Turner

The Eldership – J.W. McGarvey

With the Bishops and Deacons – James D. Cox

The Elders Which Are Among You – Bobby Duncan

Turn-Around Churches – George Barna

Good News and Bad News: A Realistic Assessment of Churches of Christ in the United States 2008 – Flavil R. Yeakley

Spiritual Sword Oct 2003 – The Model Church

Spiritual Sword July 1996 – Leadership in the Church

Biblical Eldership – Alexander Strauch

Holy Spirit Elders – Harold G. Taylor

The Elder and his Work – Robert R. Taylor, Jr

Elders and Deacons – J. B. Myers

The Eternal Kingdom – F. W. Mattox

Preparing for the Eldership – Garland Robinson

Church Leadership and Organization – Flavil Yeakley

Efficient Leadership in the Church – Goebel Music

"Leadership in the Church, Home, Government" – 17th "Seek the Old Paths" Lectureship – Garland M. Robinson, Editor

Encouraging Elders – Thomas Holland

Leadership: The Crisis of Our Time – Wendell Winkler

How to build a Great Church – Mac Layton

User Friendly Churches – George Barna

Like a Shepherd Lead Us – David Fleer & Charles Siburt

Gospel Advocate

Gospel Journal

Spiritual Sword

Christian Courier

Apologetics Press

Exhibit 3

ATTENDANCE SHEET

Absent 3 Consecutive Sundays - July 1, 8 & 15

	LAST	FIRST	W1 Sunday a.m. (1st week)	W2 Sunday a.m. (2nd week)	W3 Sunday a.m. (3rd week)	1PM Sunday p.m. (1st week)	2PM Sunday p.m. (2nd week)	3PM Sunday p.m. (3rd week)	Remarks	Letters Sent
25			A	A	A	A	A	A		
26			A	A	A	A	A	A		
48			A	A	A	A	A	A		
62			A	A	A	A	A	A		
74			A	A	A	A	A	A		
101			A	A	A	A	A	A		
116			A	A	A	A	A	A		
118			A	A	A	A	A	A		
119			A	A	A	A	A	A		
151			A	A	A	A	A	A		
175			A	A	A	A	A	A		
176			A	A	A	A	A	A		
183			A	A	A	A	A	A		
196			A	A	A	A	A	A		
239			A	A	A	A	A	A		
262			A	A	A	A	A	A		
274			A	A	A	A	A	A		
286			A	A	A	A	A	A		
287			A	A	A	A	A	A		

3rd QUARTER - July - September

Exhibit 4

First Delinquent Letter

Date

Name

Address

Dear,

We have missed seeing you at worship services the past two Sundays. This note is just to let you know that we love you and your family and hope and pray that all is well.

As elders we are responsible for your spiritual well-being and we take this task very seriously (Hebrews 13:17).

It may be that you did not complete an attendance card, sign the attendance sheet, etc. In a congregation of our size this is the only way we can be certain of your faithful attendance each week.

We hope to see you this Sunday. If we can be of service please let us know.

Yours in Christ,

The Elders

_____   _____

_____   _____

Exhibit 5

Second Delinquent Letter

Date

Name

Address

Dear,

As best we can determine you have been absent from services for at least the last three Sundays. The purpose of this letter is to let you know that we are very concerned about you. Christians have the privilege and obligation to assemble upon the first day of the week to worship God (Hebrews 10:25; Acts 20:7; 1Corinthians 16:1,2; Acts 2:42). Willfully missing the assembly is disobedient to God's command which places your soul in jeopardy. As the shepherds of the flock we are to watch for your soul and will be held accountable if we do not faithfully carry out this responsibility. (Hebrews 13:17; 1Peter 5:1,2; Acts 20:28).

If your absence is due to negligence and disobedience to God we pray that you will repent and come back home. The scriptures teach that we must withdraw ourselves from those who become unfaithful (2Thessalonians 3:6). If there is a reason for your absence that we do not know please inform us. We stand ready to help you in any way possible.

Yours in Christ,

The Elders,

_____   _____

_____   _____

Exhibit 6

THIRD DELINQUENT LETTER

Date

Name
Address

Dear,

Have you forgotten the exhortation of the Holy Spirit, "Be faithful until death and I will give you the crown of life" (Revelation 2:10)? Have you forgotten your former cleansing from your old sins (2 Peter 1:9)?

Do you remember that the Holy Spirit said through Peter, "For it would have been better for them not to have known the way of righteousness, than having known it to turn back from the holy commandment delivered to them" (2 Peter 2:21)?

(Name), we have written you, visited and talked with you and attempted to encourage you to return to faithfulness. It appears that all our efforts have been in vain. We have and will continue to pray for you because we love you and want so much to see your soul saved in eternity.

Frankly, we do not know what more to say or do. If you will tell us how we can help you live faithfully for the Lord we will do our best to make that happen. As it stands now, you are bringing reproach upon Christ and His church. This reproach is due to the fact that you know what is right, you know what the Lord wants you to do but you refuse to do it.

(Name), because of our love for you and our love for the Lord and His church we must take action to bring your name before the congregation for disciplinary action. As much as this hurts us, you have left us no choice.

You must realize the seriousness of your unfaithfulness. You are not only jeopardizing your own soul, you are encouraging others, directly or indirectly, to be unfaithful also.

Unless we hear from you by (date), we must fulfill our responsibility to the Lord and His church by bringing your name before the congregation and withdraw fellowship from you.

Please contact us, we are praying for your return.

In Christian Love,

The Elders

_____   _____

_____   _____

Exhibit 7

STATEMENTS PLACING DELINQUENT MEMBER'S NAME
BEFORE THE CONGREGATION

The fellowship between Christians is the sweetest and most vital activity that Christ gave the church to sustain us while we remain here on earth (1John 1:3). This fellowship is required by each of us. When a member of Christ's body walks disorderly, we are commanded to withhold our fellowship from them as a final means of admonishment to the wrongdoer (2Thessalonians 3:6,14,15).

The most serious and sobering duty that elders have is watching for the souls of the local congregation (Hebrews 13:17). We, the elders, must give an account for your souls. Therefore, it is imperative that we do all that God has instructed to bring back the unfaithful and at the same time protect the flock by purging sin from the body.

_____ continues to exhibit a rebellious and un-repenting attitude towards God's commands. Unless he/she is restored to faithful service and once again becomes obedient to God's law, we will have no choice but to withhold our social fellowship from him/her.

Many efforts have been made to contact him/her without success. If any member has influence with _____ or a method of reaching him/her to provide encouragement to repent and return to the church you should do so this week. Every member should diligently pray for him/her (Galatians 6:1-2,9-10).

The elders have exhausted all efforts to contact him/her. If we have no positive response by next Sunday, (Date), _____ will be considered erring and because of his/her careless and indifferent attitude, we must withhold our fellowship from him/her.

Prayer

Exhibit 7a

In overseeing the flock here at _____ the elders have the dual responsibilities of doing our utmost to keep the saved saved and maintain the purity of the church. We take both of these tasks very seriously.

We have been working with _____ for a long time attempting to strengthen him/her spiritually and encourage him/her to return to faithful service to the Lord. He/She has repented before only to fall away again. This time we have been unsuccessful in convincing him/her of his/her obligation to faithfully serve God and attend worship services.

Galatians is a general letter to all Christians directing them in chapter six verse one to restore those who have fallen away. We are again placing _____'s name before the congregation and asking that everyone pray for his/her repentance and make every effort to contact him/her. If we do not hear from _____ by next Sunday night, (Date), we will ask the congregation to formally withdraw fellowship from him/her in order to admonish _____ to return and to keep the church pure from sin.

Bow with me as we pray for _____.

Exhibit 8

STATEMENT WITHDRAWING SOCIAL FELLOWSHIP
FROM A DELINQUENT MEMBER

God has commanded Christians to live a life worthy of their calling (Ephesians 4:1; Colossians 1:10; 2 Thessalonians 2:12). This includes faithful service to God in a local congregation as well as adhering to His laws concerning our personal lives. When a brother or sister continues to live a life in rebellion to those commands we are instructed to withhold our social fellowship from them as a final means of bringing them back to the fold (1 Corinthians 5:4-6).

Last week _____'s name was put before the church because he/she has been walking disorderly. You were asked to pray for him/her and make every effort to contact him/her in an effort to bring him/her back to repentance. We trust everyone has made this effort.

There has been no response from _____. Therefore we have no choice but to follow the commandment the scriptures have given us to withhold our social fellowship from him/her as of today (Romans 16:17; 2 Thessalonians 3:6). We are not to treat him/her as an enemy, but as a brother/sister in Christ (2 Thessalonians 3:14-15). We ask that you continue to pray for him/her to come back home to Jesus and the fellowship that protects him/her.

Prayer

Exhibit 9

LETTER TO WITHDRAWN MEMBER

Dear,

We love you and continue to be very concerned about your soul's salvation. Even though the church has now withdrawn social fellowship from you because of your unfaithfulness, you are still a member of the Lord's church.

The Bible describes your spiritual condition in 2Peter 2:20-22: "For if after they have escaped the pollutions of the world through the knowledge of the Lord and Savior Jesus Christ, they are again entangled in them and overcome, the latter end is worse for them than the beginning. For it would have been better for them not to have known the way of righteousness, than having known it, to turn from the holy commandment delivered to them. But it has happened to them according to the true proverb: "A dog returns to his vomit," and "a sow, having washed, to her wallowing in the mire."

The Bible also teaches us our obligations to you in 2 Thessalonians 3:14-15: "And if anyone does not obey our word in this epistle, note that person and do not keep company with him, that he may be ashamed. Yet do not count him as an enemy, but admonish him as a brother."

We are writing this letter to you to express our love for you and to admonish you to repent and be restored to a life of faithfulness. We hope and pray that you will consider the value of your soul.

In Christ,

The Elders,

_____   _____

_____   _____

Exhibit 10

Follow Up Letter to Withdrawn Member

Dear ,

Even though we have withdrawn fellowship from you, we still continue to love you and remain deeply concerned for your soul. We encourage you to read the following passage from the Word of God: 2 Peter 2:20-22: "For if after they have escaped the pollutions of the world through the knowledge of the Lord and Savior Jesus Christ, they are again entangled in them and overcome, the latter end is worse for them than the beginning. For it would have been better for them not to have known the way of righteousness, than having known it, to turn from the holy commandment delivered to them. But it has happened to them according to the true proverb: "A dog returns to his vomit," and "a sow, having washed, to her wallowing in the mire."

This passage clearly teaches that as an unfaithful Christian your soul is in the worse possible condition. Remember, one day you will stand before Christ in judgment. Paul said in 2 Corinthians 5:10-11 "For we must all appear before the judgment seat of Christ, that each one may receive the things done in the body, whether good or bad. Knowing therefore, the terror of the Lord, we persuade men; but we are well known to God, and I also trust are well known in your consciences."

We continue to hope and pray that you will come back to Christ and His church and again become a faithful Christian. We would welcome the opportunity to meet and study with you in hope of encouraging you to make the right decision about your soul.

It is never too late to come back to the Lord while you remain on this earth. We would ask you to read the story of the Prodigal Son in Luke 15:11-32, and just as the father rejoiced when his lost son came home, there will be a great rejoicing in heaven if you decide to come back to the Lord. Our earnest desire and prayer is for you to consider all of this seriously. We stand ready to assist you, study with you or answer any questions that you may have. Please feel free to contact one of us.

May God bless you with a long life and tender heart.

In Christian love,

The Elders,

_____   _____

_____   _____

Exhibit 11

FOLLOW UP LETTER TO THE CONGREGATION CONCERNING A WITHDRAWN MEMBER

Dear Brethren,

As your elders we are responsible for every soul in this congregation and its spiritual welfare (Hebrews 13:17). When members of this congregation become unfaithful, we, as the elders, are to take the lead in attempting to restore them (Acts 20:28; 1Thessalonians 5:12-13; 1Peter 5:1-4). If after all scriptural and reasonable means have been exhausted to restore them and they still do not repent, it is our obligation to also take the lead in withdrawing fellowship from them (1Corinthians 5:1-13; 2Thessalonians 3:6-15).

On (Date), after having placed the names of _____ and _____ before the congregation and exhorting each member to seek to restore the erring to a right relationship with God, we asked the _____ congregation to withdraw fellowship in order to obey the Lord, purge the church and bring the erring to repentance.

It is the purpose of this letter to remind you of this action if you were here or to inform you of this action if you were not in the assembly on that day. Also be reminded that we are not to regard such a one as an enemy but as a brother or sister in Christ and to continue to seek to restore them (2Thessalonians 3:14, 15; Galatians 6:1, 2; James 5:19, 20).

In Christ,

The Elders,

_____   _____

_____   _____

Exhibit 12

Lessons on Church Discipline

Introduction

This study is divided into three sections:

    1. Establishing authority for discipline

    2. Instructive (preventive) discipline – teach, warn, exhort

    3. Corrective discipline – withdraw fellowship

I. **The Church is commanded (authorized) by Jesus Christ to exercise discipline**

A. Christ has all authority

1. Matt 7:28-29 – spoke with authority
2. Matt 17:1-5 -- hear Him
3. Acts 3:22-23 – hear in all things
4. Eph 1:22-23 – head over all
5. Col1:18 – preeminence
6. Matt 28:18-20 – all authority
7. Heb 1:1-2 – God speaks through Jesus
8. John 3:31,35 – above all
9. John 17:2 – all flesh
10. Col3:17 – do all in His name

B. He has placed this "all authority" in His Word

1. John 17:8, 14,17, 20-21
2. John 12:48-49

C. We must respect the Lord's all authoritative Word

1. Adam and Eve (Genesis 3)
2. Nadab and Abihu (Leviticus 10)
3. Moses (Numbers 20)

4. Uzzah (2Samuel 6 &1 Chronicles 15)

5. King Saul (1Samuel 13,15)

6. John 12:48; 1Peters 4:11

D. Church discipline is specifically connected to the authority of Christ and His Word

1. 1Corinthians 5:4,5 – In the name of our Lord Jesus Christ

2. 2Thessalonians 3:6 – In the name of our Lord Jesus Christ

3. 2Thessalonians3:14 – And if any man does not obey our word in this epistle....

II. Instructive or preventive discipline

A. Instructive discipline is to precede corrective discipline and is to actually prevent the need for it

B. What is involved in instructive (preventive) discipline?

1. All members should know that they have been born again into God's spiritual family, the church, and that they need to grow and mature as Christians (1Peter1:22-25; 1Peter 2:1-2; Hebrews 5:12;6:1; 1Corinthians 3:1-3)

2. All members need to know that they are loved and that they really belong in their spiritual family (1Corinthians12:25; Romans 13:8; Romans12:10; 1John 3:18)

3. All members need responsibility in the church (1Corinthians 15:58; Titus 3:1; Matthew 21:28-32)

4. Members need watchful guidance by elders (Acts 20:28; Hebrews 13:17)

5. However, preventive discipline does not remove the personal responsibility each individual Christian has to grow, develop, and stay faithful (1Corinthians 9:24-27; Philippians 2:12; Romans 14:12)

6. Preventive discipline therefore includes self-discipline of each individual member (Matthew16:24)

7. Growth involves: Food (1Peter 2:2), Exercise (1Timothy 4:7-8), Environment (1Corinthians15:33, Time (Hebrews5:12– 14)

III. Corrective Discipline – withdrawal of fellowship

A. When a Christian lacks self-discipline and fails to respond to instructive and preventive discipline, he falls away and becomes unfaithful

B. The Church, under the leadership of the elders, should try to restore such a person to faithfulness
   1. Warn (1Thessalonians5:14)
   2. Convert (James 5:19-20)
   3. Restore (Galatians 6:1-2)

C. When these efforts fail the church must withdraw fellowship from the unfaithful

D. Withdrawing fellowship is a command of God:
   1. Matthew 18:15-17
   2. 1Corinthians 5:1-13
   3. 2Thessalonians 3:6-15
   4. 2John 9-11
   5. Romans 16:17-18
   6. Titus 3:10-11

E. Withdrawing fellowship is necessary:
   1. To obey the Lord
   2. To restore the erring (1Corinthians 5:4-5; 2Thessalonians 3:14)
   3. To keep the church pure and save the souls of other members (1Corinthians 5:6)
   4. To save the world (Philippians 2:14-16; Acts 5:11)

F. Withdrawing fellowship involves:
   1. "Mark"/"avoid" (Romans16:17-18)
   2. "Purge out" (1Corinthians 5:7)
   3. "Not to company" (1Corinthians 5:9)
   4. "Not even eat with such a person (1Corinthians5:11)

5. "Withdraw yourselves" (2Thessalonians 3:6)

6. "Note that man, and have no company with him" (2Thessalonians 3:14)

7. "Reject" (Titus3:10-11)

8. "Do not receive him into your house" (2John 9-11)

9. The ONLY contact we should have should be to admonish that person as a brother or sister in Christ (2Thessalonians3:14,-15)

G. We must withdraw from:

1. Those that walk disorderly (2Thessalonians 3:6-15)

2. Those that engage in sinful acts (II Tim 3:1-5; 1Corinthians 5:1-13)

3. Those that teach error (Romans16:17; 2John 9-11; Titus 3:10-11)

4. Troublemakers (1Timothy 6:3-5)

5. The idle, busybodies (2Thessalonians 3:6-15)

6. Those who cause division and offences (Romans 16:17-18)

7. Those who will not be admonished (Matthew18:15-17)

8. Those who will not follow the teachings of the apostles (2Thessalonians3:14-15)

H. The elders should take the lead in this action, but the whole church must administer and support this action (1Corinthians 5:4; Hebrews 13:17)

I. If the erring repent, then the faithful should receive that person back into full fellowship (2Corinthians 2:6-8; Luke 17:3; Acts 8:22)

Exhibit 13

INVITATION LETTER TO DEACON'S CLASS

Dear (husband and wife),

Recently you were invited to attend a preparatory deacon's class we will be teaching on Wednesday nights for the fall quarter. This letter is a reminder of that invitation.

We recognize our duty to prepare future leaders at this congregation and have developed this class with that goal in mind. While there is no set timetable or guaranty concerning your being asked to accept the office of deacon, we want to ensure that you understand the qualifications and responsibilities that come with this office before the need arises.

We will remain a strong congregation only as long as we have strong leadership. We need men who know the book and are willing to take a stand for the Lord. We need men who have counted the cost and are willing to pay the price to serve God to the best of their abilities. We believe you have the potential to meet those qualifications.

We look forward to seeing you on (date).

In Christ,

The Elders

_____   _____

_____   _____

PROSPECTIVE DEACON'S CLASS

I. Introduction

    a. Why this class is necessary

    b. Why you were invited

    c. Importance of leaders

    d. Training and development of prospective deacons

V. Office of Deacon

    a. Meaning of the word "deacon"

    b. Work of deacons (Acts 6:1-6)

    c. Examples of deacons assisting elders: worship, teaching, visiting, benevolence, facilities, grounds, youth, publications, involvement, finances, missions, transportation, seniors, widows/elderly, care groups

IV. Qualifications of deacons (I Timothy 3:8-13)

V. Outies - ministry descriptions, meetings, reporting, review

VI. Selection/appointment

Exhibit 14

PROSPECTIVE DEACON DISCUSSION OUTLINE

Introduction

I.   Need for leaders

II. Identifying potential leaders
- a. Bible qualifications (1Timothy 3:8-13)
- b. Bible knowledge
- c. Faithfulness
- d. Secular/Spiritual maturity
- e. Family
- f. Life style
- g. Dependability
- h. Stewardship
- i. Involvement/Initiative

III. Preparing potential leaders
- a. Classes
- b. Ministry assignments
- c. Outside reading/seminars

IV. Supporting the Eldership
- a.   Internal ministries
- b.   Programs
  - Foster care/adoption organization
  - Children's home
  - Lads to Leaders
  - Missionaries
  - Gospel meetings
- c. Doctrinal positions
  - Marriage/divorce/remarriage
  - Smoking
  - Social drinking
  - Modesty
  - Deacon's questionnaire

d. Ministries/Programs you do not support?

V. Deacon responsibilities
   a. Attend monthly meetings
   b. Visit your widow once a month
   c. Attend activities/events
   d. Diligently work in your assigned ministry
   e. Keep your overseeing elder informed
   f. Be a continual example to the flock in living for Christ

VII. Proposed ministry assignment

VIII. Questions for elders/installation date

IX. Prayer/Close

Exhibit 15

Questionnaire for Deacons, Teachers, Preachers, Guest Speakers, Short-Term and Long-Term Missionaries Associated with the _____ Church of Christ

Name: _____ Congregation: _____

Address: _____ Date: _____

_____ E-Mail: _____

Phone: _____

Please circle Yes or No or N/A

1. Do you believe the Bible is the complete, verbally inspired Word of God and is inerrant, absolute and knowable by man (2 Timothy 3:16-17; 1 Thessalonians 2:13) **Yes or No?**

2. Do you believe the Bible is the only absolute standard for determining right from wrong? (Romans 10:17; 2 Timothy 3:16) **Yes or No?**

3. Do you believe the New Testament is our sole source of authority from God to act in religious matters (Hebrews 8:13; Galatians 3:24; Hebrews 12:24) **Yes or No?**

4. Do you believe God created the heavens and earth and all living things in six (24 hour) days (Genesis 1; Exodus 20:11) **Yes or No?**

5. Do you believe God destroyed all mankind, except Noah and his family, and all things living on land or that flew in the air, except those on the ark, in a universal flood (Genesis 7) **Yes or No?**

6. Do you believe the Bible teaches that the kingdom of God on earth and the church are one in the same and that the church was established on the day of Pentecost (Matthew 16:18,19; Colossians

1;13; Revelation 1:9; Acts 2:47; Ephesians 1:22; Colossians 1:18; John 3:5) **Yes or No?**

7. Do you believe the Bible teaches there is only one church whose head is Christ and only those who are baptized into Christ are added to that one church by God (Ephesians 4:4; 5:23; Acts 2:47; Galatians 3:27) **Yes or No?**

8. Do you believe the Bible teaches that all who have reached the "age of accountability" are separated from God because of their sins (Isaiah 59:2; Romans 3:23) **Yes or No?**

9. Do you believe the Bible teaches that in order for a soul to be saved that soul must have faith in Christ and His Word, repent of sin, confess with their mouth that Jesus is the Son of God, and be immersed in water for the remission of sins? At that point God adds that soul to the one church revealed in the pages of the New Testament (Romans 10:17; Hebrews 11:6; Matthew 10:32,33; Romans 10:9,10; Acts 2:38; 3:17; 17:30; 22:16; Mark 16:16; Romans 6:1-4; Galatians 3:26-27) **Yes or No?**

10. Do you believe the Bible teaches that all spiritual blessings are in Christ and if we turn away from Him after we have known and obeyed Him, the spiritual blessings (eternal life) will be taken away (Ephesians 1:3; 2Peter 2:21) **Yes or No?**

11. Do you believe the Bible teaches only one kind of music is to be used in worship to God and this is singing? Anything else, such as playing mechanical instruments, clapping, humming or imitating musical instruments with our mouth, is not commanded and is not pleasing to God in our worship to Him? There is no example for choirs, solos or singing groups in worship to God since we are to speak **to one another** in psalms, hymns, and spiritual songs (Colossians 3:16; Ephesians 5:19; Matthew 7:21-23) **Yes or No?**

12. Do you believe the Bible teaches that the Lord's Supper is to be taken only on the first day of the week and every first day of the week as part of our worship to God (1 Corinthians 11:23-26; Acts 20:7) **Yes or No?**

13. Do you believe the Bible teaches that women are not to lead prayer, teach or have authority over Christian men (1Corinthians 14:34; 1Timothy 2:11-12; Titus 2:3-5) **Yes or No?**

14. Do you believe the Bible teaches that the Holy Spirit, which enabled first century Christians to perform miracles to confirm the Word, no longer works in this manner? This is because we have the complete will of God and the apostles and those to whom they imparted spiritual gifts have died (Acts 8:18; 1Corinthians 13:8-10) **Yes or No?**

15. Do you believe the Bible teaches that the church is to withdraw fellowship from those in the church who walk disorderly? The purpose of the withdrawal is to attempt to restore them to faithful service and to purge sin from the church (2Thessalonians 3:6,14; 1Timothy 6:3-5; 1Corinthians 5:7, 9-13) **Yes or No?**

16. Do you believe the Bible teaches that false teachers and those who receive and fellowship them and any works they promote, such as lectureships or workshops, are to be avoided by Christians (2John 9-11; Romans 16:17,18; Titus 1:9-11; 2Timothy 4:3) **Yes or No?**

17. Do you believe the Bible teaches that marriage is for life and that the only scriptural reason for divorce and remarriage is adultery? Then the only one free to remarry is the innocent party. If the guilty party remarries he/she commits adultery. (Matthew 5:32; 19:9; Luke 16:18; Mark 10:2-12) **Yes or No?**

18. Do you believe the wearing of (short) shorts; swimsuits or other similar attire (by men or women) in public is NOT in keeping with Christian modesty? **Yes or No?** If not, please explain below.

19. Do you abstain from drinking alcoholic beverages? **Yes or No?** If not, please explain below why you believe this is acceptable.

20. Do you abstain from using tobacco products or illegal drugs? **Yes or No?** If not, please explain below why you believe this is acceptable.

21. Do you agree while working with a missionary in the field, to defer to his decisions in matters of judgment/discretion? **Yes or No or N/A?**

If you answered No to any of the above questions, please provide a brief explanation for your uncertainty. If you wish to discuss any of these matters with us privately, please let us know.

Thank you for your cooperation.

In Christian love,

The Elders

_____

_____

_____

_____

_____

_____

_____

_____

Signature: _____

22. Do you believe the Bible teaches that elders have the final authority in making decisions that pertain to the optional matters of the local congregation? (Acts 14:23; 20:7; Titus 1:5) **Yes or No?**

23. Do you believe Christians should pay their debts? **Yes or No?**

24. Do you avoid using profane words or words that are not in keeping with Christian character? **Yes or No?**

25. Do you believe it is unacceptable for a Christian to dance in public? **Yes or No?** If no, please explain below.

26. Do you believe Christians should NOT engage in mixed swimming? **Yes or No?** If no, please explain below.

27. Do you believe a Christian should attend every worship service of the congregation that is possible? **Yes or No?** If not, please explain below.

28. Do you attend every worship service possible? **Yes or No?**

29. Do your children attend every worship service possible? **Yes or No?**

30. Do you attempt to attend every service possible of Gospel Meetings, Vacation Bible Schools or other efforts? **Yes or No?**

31. Do you believe and support gospel preaching that involves rebuking, reproving and exhorting? **Yes or No?**

32. How do you decide how much to give on the first day of the week?
    _____
    _____

33. Will you always try to be Christ-like? **Yes or No?**

34. Will you strive to keep down church cliques? **Yes or No?**

35. Will you, if you change your mind on any of the above questions, promptly notify the elders? **Yes or No?**

If you answered **No** to any of questions 19-35, please provide a brief explanation about your uncertainty. If you wish to discuss any of these matters with us privately, please let us know.

Thank you for your cooperation.

In Christian love,

The Elders

_____

_____

_____

_____

_____

_____

_____

_____

Signature: _____

Exhibit 16

Annual Deacon Commitment Questionnaire
(Year)

Please circle Yes or No

1. Will you effectively perform the responsibilities given to you by the elders? **Yes/No?**

2. Will you make every effort to attend all monthly deacons' meetings as well as any other meetings called by the elders? If for any reason you are unable to do so, will you notify the chairperson that you will not be attending? **Yes/No?**

3. If assigned a widow, will you complete your monthly visitation assignment as outlined by the elders? **Yes/No?**

4. Will you do everything possible to support our current programs and any new programs being presented to the congregation in (year), which are designed to promote spiritual and numerical growth of the church? **Yes/No?**

5. Will you faithfully attend worship services, and gospel meetings? **Yes/No?**

6. If, at any time, you feel that you cannot be effective or perform your responsibilities as a deacon, will you submit your resignation to the elders? **Yes/No?**

My assigned elder is _____.

Deacon's Signature: _____.

Date: _____

Exhibit 17

DEACON NOMINATION PROCEDURES

1. Read Acts 6:1-4 to the congregation

2. Read the following statement: "Due to the growth of our congregation and/or recent turnover in our deacons, the elders have recognized the need for additional men to be appointed to this office. We have selected (#) men for your consideration."

3. Read their names and ask the man and wife to stand.

4. Explain the proposed responsibilities of this office.

5. Read the following statement: "If anyone in the congregation knows of a scriptural reason why any of these men should not be appointed to the office of deacon, we would ask that you submit a signed statement to the elders outlining your reasons, by this (date). If we do not receive a response, we intend to install these men next Sunday (date)".

6. Prayer

Exhibit 18

DEACON INSTALLATION PROCEDURES

1. Read the following statement: "Last Sunday the names of _____, _____, _____, were placed before the congregation for your consideration as deacons. We have not received any scriptural reasons why any of these men should not be appointed; therefore we will install them this morning."

2. Read 1Timothy 3:8-13

3. Ask the men and their wives to stand as you call their names.

4. Ask the following question of the man: "Do you understand the qualifications and accept the responsibilities of the office of deacon in the Lord's church at _____ congregation?"

5. Ask the following question of the wife: "Do you understand the qualifications and accept the responsibilities as a deacon's wife?"

6. Read the names of the men appointed as deacons.

7. Prayer

Exhibit 19

ELDER/DEACON ASSIGNMENTS (YEAR)

Smith	Jones	Doe	Ward
Local Outreach	Missions	Delinquents	Bible School
Gospel Meetings	Finances	Worship	Lads to Leaders
Transportation	Office Staff	Benevolence	Youth
Involvement	Printing	Visitation	Care Groups
Bldg/Grounds	Correspondence		

Deacon	Assignment	Widow	Elder
White	Transportation	Ester	Smith
Brown	Benevolence	Pearl	Doe

Exhibit 20

<u>   </u> CHURCH OF CHRIST

DEACON'S MINISTRY DESCRIPTIONS

Ministry: Building Maintenance

Objective: Maintain the structural integrity and functionality of all buildings to include all internal support systems such as electrical, mechanical, plumbing, heating and air conditioning.

Responsibilities: Deacon will perform and/or coordinate, in a timely manner the tasks necessary to maintain our buildings in good working order and appearance. This excludes maintenance of the sound system and printing equipment which are covered under other ministries. Close coordination with the church secretaries is expected. Routine work should be accomplished by volunteer church members, if feasible, to reduce expenditures. A joint decision by the deacon and his overseeing elder will be made as to the need for professional services on complex technical projects. A dollar limit will be established by the overseeing elder concerning deacon-only approval of professional third party services. Congregational work days will be scheduled, as necessary, to accomplish routine cleanup and/or repairs.

Ministry: Bible School Director

Objective: Organize and administer an effective Bible education program for our members

Responsibilities: Deacon will accomplish, as a minimum, the following duties:

1. Develop a draft curriculum for the primary, secondary and adult classes to include topics, materials, teachers, classrooms and a rolling quarterly schedule for the next three years. This plan will be reviewed and approved by the elders each year.

2. Conduct quarterly coordinators/teachers meetings to discuss teaching assignments, materials, special events, etc.

3. Monitor classes for teacher/material effectiveness.

4. Pray daily for the teachers and students.

5. Prepare an annual budget for the elders.

6. Recruit and train prospective teachers to include discussing prospects with your overseeing elder before contacting the prospect, obtaining a completed teacher questionnaire and placing them in a teaching assignment.

7. Evaluate and approve requests for class material and supplies. Assure these items are promptly ordered and delivered.

8. Plan the annual Vacation Bible School (VBS) to include the selection of topics, materials, song leaders, awards, refreshments, teachers and assistants.

9. Provide assistance to department coordinators such as direction, mediation and logistics.

Ministry: Youth

Objective: Develop and administer a program to actively involve our youth in Christian activities that will foster a sense of unity within the group and promote Christian values.

Responsibilities: Deacon will accomplish the following:

1. Recruit, develop and coordinate participation of individuals and couples to assist in the youth program (teen and pre-teen).

2. Oversee development and implementation of an annual schedule of activities and service projects.

3. Assign responsibilities to coordinators for various activities and provide them with the resources necessary to carry out those activities.

4. Meet with all new families with children to discuss the youth program and encourage their active participation.

5. Prepare an annual youth budget in coordination with your overseeing elder.

6. Plan and execute quarterly youth coordinators meetings to ensure the program is meeting its objectives.

7. Continually encourage the congregation in general and families with children in particular, by visiting the youth classes, publishing a calendar of events, maintaining the bulletin board, including information on Power Point.

8. Maintain an awareness of church-wide youth activities and those that would be appropriate for our youth.

Ministry: Benevolence

Objective: Provide material blessings to members and non-members on an "as needed" basis in accordance with guidelines established by the elders.

Responsibilities: Deacon will accomplish the following:

1. Receive and investigate requests made to the church for assistance regarding food, money, etc.

    a. Reasonable requests from non-church members will be handled without contacting the elders. This assistance consists primarily of food and money within limits established by the elders.

    b. Requests from members of the church will be referred to the elders for investigation and decisions on the extent of assistance.

    c. Cash will not be given directly to those seeking assistance in most cases. If it is determined that a bill will be paid by the church, the check will be sent directly to the company to whom the debt is owed, such as the gas, electric, water companies, rent or mortgage payments, prescriptions, etc.

2. Supervise the food pantry and food coupons to include inventory and distribution. Those people making repetitive and/or unreasonable requests that appear to be abusing the program will be referred to the elders.

3. Your primary responsibility is to ensure that the Lord's resources are used wisely. The person must have the confidence and support of the elders.

Exhibit 21

GUIDELINES FOR WIDOWS AND THE ELDERLY

It is the responsibility of the church to care for its members. Widows and the elderly may require continual assistance at some level to maintain a reasonable quality of life and active involvement in worship and church related functions. There are four categories of people to which these guidelines relate:

1. True widows in deed (1 Timothy 5:5)

2. Widows with believing children (1 Timothy 5:16)

3. Widows with unbelieving children

4. Elderly who need assistance

Widows with believing children are to be cared for by those children according to 1 Timothy 5:4,16. Other widows and elderly members will be assigned to a deacon. Each deacon is expected to visit their widow in their home at least once each month for the purpose of developing a trusting relationship with them and to determine if spiritual or material assistance is needed. The deacon will perform or coordinate performance of routine maintenance of their widow's dwelling, vehicle, etc. Projects involving church funds will be coordinated with the deacon's overseeing elder. Deacons will report on the status of their widows at the monthly elders/deacons meetings.

Exhibit 22

ANNUAL DEACON'S RETREAT AGENDA

Chairman: _____

Secretary: _____

Devotional: _____

Attendees: _____

_____

I.   Discussion items requested by the elders:
        a.
        b.
        c.

II.   Old business
        a.
        b.
        c.

III.   Deacons ministry reports
        a. Bible school
        b. Building and grounds

VI.   New business
        a.
        b.
        c.

V.   Miscellaneous items
        a.
        b.
        c.

VI. Close

Exhibit 23

TERMS OF OVERSIGHT AGREEMENT - MISSIONARIES

Date

Vacation: The elders and (Missionary Name) agree that he will have two weeks' vacation each year that he is working under the elders' oversight. (Missionary Name) will be paid his normal salary during these weeks. Expenses incurred by him and/or his family during this time, such as transportation or recreation, that are directly related to their vacation will be paid out of his personal funds, not his work or special projects funds.

Termination: The elders and (missionary name) agree that either party may terminate their relationship by providing ninety days' notice of intended termination. Financial support and oversight will continue during these ninety days. Funds remaining in the general, work and special projects accounts will be disbursed to (missionary name) and/or his supporting congregations at the elders' discretion.

Elders:

_____   _____
(printed name)   (printed name)

_____   _____
(printed name)   (printed name)

Missionary:

_____   Date: _____
(printed name)

Exhibit 24

PACKING LIST

Laptop	___	Projector	___
Sermons	___	Sermon outlines	___
Passport	___	Passport holder	___
Visa	___	Lysol	___
Speaking permit	___	Calculator	___
Cash	___	Insect spray	___
Traveler's checks	___	Reading glasses	___
Sun glasses	___	Sandals	___
Personal Bible study aids	___	Family photo	___
Bible	___	Vitamins	___
Camera	___	Medication(s)	___
Flip flops	___	Journal	___
Laundry bag	___	Ibuprofen	___
Snacks	___	Nail clippers	___
Toiletries	___	Reading light	___
Reading book	___	Note pad	___
Tickets	___	Student list	___
Cough drops	___	Pens/Pencils	___

Coffee	____	Phone card	____
Batteries	____	Travel converter	____
3x5 cards	____	Alarm clock	____
Watch	____	Shirts	____
Socks	____	Shoes	____
Band Aids	____	Belts	____
Slacks	____	Jacket	____
Flashlight	____	Tennis shoes	____
Shorts	____	Ties	____
Travel iron	____	Umbrella	____
CD's/DVD's	____	Headphones	____
T-shirts	____	Shampoo	____
Ready ref book	____	Hand wash	____
Denominational doctrine info	____	Gatorade power	____
Sunscreen	____	Ice pack	____
Handy wipes	____	Cell phone	____
Neosporin	____	Cell charger	____
Bibles	____	Toilet tissue	____
Tums	____	Pillow	____
Soap/container	____	Immunization shots	____

Exhibit 25

Preparation for Short-Term Missionary Campaigns

Introduction

Scriptural work of the church

Good stewards of our time, effort and money

The 5 P's apply "Proper Preparation Prevents Poor Performance"

Murphy's Law also applies!

I. Long-term Planning

a. Team leadership determination (elders/primary missionary)

b. Site Selection
    i. Purpose
    ii. Personnel requirements/resources (teen policy)
    iii. Cost/Financial resources
    iv. Transportation (travel restrictions/requirements)
    v. Lodging
    vi. Local conditions (transportation, food, health care/disease, government)

c. Time Frame(s)
    i. Weather
    ii. Flight availability
    iii. Follow-up team
    iv. School year considerations

d. Training
    i. Schedule
    ii. Agenda

e. Milestones
    i. Date of announcement to congregation
    ii. Date to start training

II. Training/Preparation

a. Initial Meeting (18 months out)
    i. Purpose of monthly meetings (training, preparation, unity)

    ii. Destination

    iii. Time frame(s)

    iv. Transportation

    v. Personnel requirements (teen policy)

    vi. Training schedule

    vii. Teaching aids

    viii. Financial requirements

    ix. Appoint secretary

    x. Insurance (medical/trip)

    xi. Passports/visas

    xii. Immunizations

    xiii. Correspondence course (CC) support (program training)

    xiv. Attendees list

    xv. Missionary overview (local customs, culture, conditions, religions)

b. Monthly Training Meetings (approaching leave date)

    i. Attendance record

    ii. Distribute minutes from last meeting and updated personnel list

    iii. Review of basics, previous meeting notes

    iv. Distribute CC student names/target cites close to base/ maintain records

    v. In-depth study of local culture

    vi. Survey of local denominational doctrines

    vii. Provide general teaching assignments for men in upcoming meetings (5th meeting)

    viii. Two men present 15 minute talks on pre-assigned personal Bible study topics

    ix. Completion of individual missionary doctrinal questionnaires

    x. Discuss correspondence course student responses and handout new response cards from potential CC students

    xi. Separate men and women with separate speaking assignments after monthly general sessions (12 months out)

    xii. Discuss on-site security issues

    xiii. Plan long-term follow up (continuing support for local congregation)

    xiv. Discuss use of e-mail to communicate with students

    xv. Assign one-on-one teaching topics/teams (6 months out)

xvi. Mail Bibles, flyers, material, etc to secure site in-country, take masters to reproduce in-county if necessary (3 months out)

xvii. Provide specific list of recommended immunizations

xviii. Discuss use of caution when communicating with students (check with leader/missionary on sensitive subjects)

xix. Provide on-site sermon, devo, prayer and song leading assignments

xx. Provide on-site daily schedule to include alternate plan to generate studies if CC's fail and possible youth activities (VBS?)

xxi. Plan transition with follow-up team (minimum 1-day overlap if possible)

xxii. Last notification to students prior to arrival on-site (1-2 months out)

xxiii. Prepare letters to mail upon arrival in country

xxiv. Informal Saturday meeting (local food from mission site)

c. Preparation

i. Finances (periodic deposits to travel account, policy on individual solicitations for support, support from general funds, plea to congregation, conversion rate)

ii. Administrative (passports, visas, tickets, lodging reservations, immunization info, insurance (health, trip), speaking permits, packing list)

iii. When making airline arrangements, allow extra "layover" time between flights to cover unforeseen delays

iv. Missionary will make on-site preparations at campaign location to include transportation from airport to hotel, advanced check-in, local transportation, meeting rooms, restaurants, banks, post office, medical facilities, phone service, interpreters, a/v equipment, baptism area, etc.

d. Departure

i. Team will be provided a last minute "critical item" checklist to include passport, visa, airline ticket, speaking permits (if required), medical supplies, recommended "carry-on" items such as jewelry, money, important documents, personal hygiene products, short term clothing, "could you function effectively if your luggage were lost?", departure time/location, etc.

    ii. Allow extra travel and check-in time to deal with unforeseen events.

e. Arrival

    i. Team leaders/missionary will ensure that team members are prepared for the customs process to include completion of appropriate forms and possible inspection of luggage

    ii. Missionary will ensure transportation is available upon arrival

    iii. Depending on the length of the flight(s) and time zones (International Date Line) crossed, allow the team to "recover" from jet lag before commencing activities

    iv. Local mailing of arrival notices to CC students

f. On-site daily activities

    i. Begin each day (other than Sunday) with a team meeting after breakfast. The agenda will include:

        1. Opening prayer

        2. Short devotional

        3. General comments and Q&A by team leaders and missionary

        4. Team member reports to include review of yesterday's activity; status of PBS's, plans for that day, misc. comments/suggestions

    ii. If the campaign goal is to plant a congregation or to create numerical growth in an existing congregation through local evangelism, the daily routines would be similar:

        1. Make contact with CC students by phone or in person and attempt to set up PBS's.

        2. Attempt to set up PBS's with people at the hotel, restaurant, bank, etc. with whom there is repeated contact.

        3. Pass out literature in public areas and/or go door nocking in neighborhoods (missionary must ensure this activity is allowed by local law and/or custom). Ensure team leader is aware of individual local travel AT ALL TIMES.

    iii. If the campaign goal is to edify a local congregation, attempt to schedule personal and/or group Bible studies on various subjects relating to that goal. These may be done at the hotel or in someone's home.

iv. Activities listed in f-ii above can be planned and executed as time permits.

v. Evening activities may include group viewing of DVD's (Jule Miller), Q&A sessions and/or classes for men, women, children and teens on various subjects appropriate for the campaign goal.

vi. Participants in Sunday worship should be scheduled beforehand along with arrangements for the location, seating, etc.

vii. Prior to the arrival of the follow-up team a meeting should be held to discuss the transition of activities to ensure a seamless handoff.

viii. A pre-departure meeting will be held to discuss clearing the hotel, transportation to the airport and out-country procedures to include necessary documentation, money conversion, tickets, etc.

ix. Schedule an "after trip" meeting within two weeks of return to discuss lessons learned. Update preparation/execution outline based on experiences.

Exhibit 26

VISITORS REPORT

Date _____

Name _____

Address _____

_____

Phone # _____

Pertinent information

Family members _____

Employment _____

Church affiliation _____

General observations _____

_____

_____

Exhibit 27

Visitors Follow-Up Report

Date   _____

Name   _____

Address _____

  _____

Phone # _____

Call completed: Yes _____   No _____

Visit competed: Yes _____   No _____

Pertinent information

Family _____

Employment _____

Church affiliation _____

General observations _____

_____

_____

Exhibit 28

COMMUNITY INVOLVEMENT REPORT

Month _____

Activities scheduled:

1. _____

2. _____

3. _____

4. _____

Activities in progress:

1. _____

2. _____

3. _____

4. _____

Activities completed in previous month:

1. _____

2. _____

3. _____

4. _____

Misc. _____

_____

Exhibit 29

New Members Orientation Class Outline

I. Directory review

II. Review of deacon/teacher/missionary questionnaire
(Exhibit 15)

III. Ministry review

    a. Joe Smith – Elder (Picture)

      i. Missions/Mission Forum
          Deacons: _____ (Pictures)
      ii. Finances
          Deacon: _____ (Picture)
      iii. Office
          Secretary: _____ (Picture)
      iv. Printing
          Deacon: _____ (Picture)

    b. Jim Long – Elder (Picture)

      i. Delinquents
          Deacon: _____ (Picture)
      ii. Worship

          Preacher: _____ (Picture)

          Assoc. Preacher: _____ (Picture)

          Deacon (scheduling): _____ (Picture)

          Deacon (announcements): _____ (Picture)

          Deacon (song leading): _____ (Picture)
      iii. Benevolence
          Deacon: _____ (Picture)
      iv. Ushers
          Deacon: _____ (Picture)

      v. Visitation
          Deacon: _____ (Picture)

c. Bob Jones – Elder (Picture)

  i.   Bible school
       Deacon (director): _____ (Picture)
       Deacon (coordinator): _____ (Picture)
       Adult classes (Sunday): _____, _____
       Adult classes (Wednesday): _____, _____

  ii. Youth
       Deacon: _____ (Picture)

  iii. Care groups
       Deacon: _____ (Picture)

            Group #1 leader: _____ (Picture)

            Group #2 leader: _____ (Picture)

            Group #3 leader: _____ (Picture)

            Group #4 leader: _____ (Picture)

  iv. Correspondence

d. Stan Brooks – Elder (Picture)

  i.   Local outreach
       Deacon/Preacher (coord.): _____ (Picture)

            Bible coor.courses: _____ (Picture)

            Greeters: _____ (Picture)

            Follow-up groups: _____ (Picture)

            Prison ministry: _____ (Picture)

            Bible studies: _____ (Picture)

            Seniors: _____ (Picture)

  ii. Gospel meetings

  iii. Transportation
       Deacon: _____ (Picture)

  iv. Involvement
       Deacon: _____ (Picture)

  v.   Building/Grounds
       Deacon: _____ (Picture)

VI. Review of involvement profile (Exhibit 30)

Exhibit 30

INVOLVEMENT PROFILE

Date: ____/____/_____

Name: _____ Phone: ____-____-_____

E-mail address: _____

Ministry/Area	Experience	Active	Interest (X)
Worship			
Preach	_____	_____	_____
Prayer	_____	_____	_____
Bible reading	_____	_____	_____
Lord's Supper	_____	_____	_____
Usher	_____	_____	_____
Greeter	_____	_____	_____
Announcements	_____	_____	_____
Song leading	_____	_____	_____
Audio/Visual	_____	_____	_____
Education			
Primary (Sunday)	_____	_____	_____
Secondary (Sunday)	_____	_____	_____
Senior (Sunday)	_____	_____	_____
Adult (Sunday)	_____	_____	_____
Primary (Wed)	_____	_____	_____
Secondary (Wed)	_____	_____	_____
Senior (Wed)	_____	_____	_____
Adult (Wed)	_____	_____	_____
Lads to Leaders	_____	_____	_____

VBS

    Teach   _____   _____   _____

    Construction   _____   _____   _____
    (Theme)

Building

    Security   _____

    Painting   _____

    Electrical   _____

    Plumbing   _____

    Carpentry   _____

    General cleaning   _____

    Changing sign   _____

    Misc.   _____

Grounds

    Yard work   _____

    Lawn mowing   _____

Benevolence

    Prepare meals   _____

    Deliver meals   _____

    Pantry   _____

    Clothing drive   _____

    Disaster relief   _____

    Transportation   _____

    Baby sitting   _____

    Care Group   _____

    Visitation/Fellowship program   _____

Specialized Skills

    Computer/Information systems   _____

    A/V operations   _____

Misc.

Bulletin boards   _____

Teacher resource room   _____

Library   _____

Bible correspondence courses   _____

Nursery attendant   _____

Office work   _____

Youth   _____

Special events   _____

Exhibit 31

LIFE GROUP COMMITTEES & CHAIRPERSON(S)

1. **Activities** (2): _____, _____

Plan activities for the group such as dinners at church, visits to shut-ins, entertainment/recreation, etc. Coordinate events at the church building with the chairperson of the set-up and clean-up committee.

2. **Bread Basket** (meals)(2): _____, _____

Help prepare meals for individuals or families in need, especially when the wife/mother is sick or in the hospital or someone has a prolonged illness. Also when there is a birth or death in the immediate family.

3. **Set-up & Clean-up** (1): _____

Responsible for setting up tables, chairs, etc in the fellowship hall or other meeting places. The rooms must be set back up as they were before the function (classes, etc), and the floors swept and mopped if necessary. The same procedure applies if the kitchen is used.

4. **Showers** (Wedding or Baby)(2): _____, _____

Plan and execute showers to include date, time, place, food, etc. Schedule use of the fellowship hall with the office.

5. **Telephone/E-mail** (2): _____, _____

Contact members about special group meetings, events, etc. Make special effort to include new members.

6. **Transportation** (1): _____

Provide transportation to group members to such places as church services, social functions, appointments, etc.

7. **Welcome to the Group** (1): _____

Invite new members into your home or out to eat. Consider inviting other members so the new family can develop social relationships as quickly as possible.

8. **Other:** _____

Exhibit 32

Life Group Profile

Name: _____ Occupation: _____

Home Phone: _____/_____/_____ Work Phone: _____/_____/_____

Pager/Cell Phone: _____/_____/_____ E-mail: _____

I would like to participate in:

_____ **Activities:** Plan activities for the group such as dinners at church, visits to shut-ins, entertainment/recreation, etc. Coordinate events at the church building with the chairperson of the set-up and clean-up committee.

_____ **Bread Basket(meals):** Help prepare meals for individuals or families in need, especially when the wife/mother is sick or in the hospital or someone has a prolonged illness. Also when there is a birth or death in the immediate family.

_____ **Set-up & Clean-up after activities:** Responsible for setting up tables, chairs, etc in the fellowship hall or other meeting places. The rooms must be set back up as they were before the function (classes, etc), and the floors swept and mopped if necessary. The same procedure applies if the kitchen is used.

_____ **Showers (Wedding & Baby):** Plan and execute showers to include date, time, place, food, etc. Schedule use of the fellowship hall with the office.

_____ **Telephone/E-mail:** Contact members about special group meetings, events, etc. Make special effort to include new members.

_____ **Transportation:** Provide transportation to group members to such places as church services, social functions, appointments, etc.

_____ **Welcome to Group:** Invite new members into your home or out to eat. Consider inviting other members so the new family can develop social relationships as quickly as possible.

Exhibit 33

ACTIVITIES

Chairpersons: _____, _____

_____

Name	Phone/E-mail

1. _____   _____

2. _____   _____

Bread Basket (Meals)

Chairpersons: _____, _____

_____

Name	Phone/E-mail

1. _____   _____

2. _____   _____

Exhibit 34

BIBLE SCHOOL
ORGANIZATIONAL CHART

Elder
Responsible for
Education

Bible School
Director

Teacher Training & Recruiting Coordinator	Cradle Roll Coordinator	Pre-School Coordinator	Primary Coordinator	High School Coor. (Sun)	VBS Coordinator	High School Coor. (Wed)	Adult Coordinator
	0-12 months Sunday	2 yr old Sunday	1st Grade Sunday	4th-6th Grade Boys (Sun)		4th-6th Grade Boys (Wed)	Auditorium Sunday
	0-12 months Wednesday	2 yr old Wednesday	1st Grade Wednesday	4th-6th Grade Girls (Sun)		4th-6th Grade Girls (Wed)	Fellowship Hall (Sun)
	12-18 months Sunday	3 yr old Sunday	2nd Grade Sunday	7th-8th Grade Sunday		7th-8th Grade Boys (Wed)	Basic Bible Class (Sun)
	12-18 months Wednesday	3 yr old Wednesday	2nd Grade Wednesday	9th-11th Grade Sunday		7th-8th Grade Girls (Wed)	Intermediate Bible Class
	18-24 months Sunday	4 yr old Sunday	3rd Grade Sunday	12th Grade Sunday		9th-12th Grade Boys (Wed)	Auditorium Wednesday
	18-24 months Wednesday	4 yr old Wednesday	3rd Grade Wednesday			9th-12th Grade Girls (Wed)	Fellowship Hall (Wed)
		5 yr old Sunday/Wed					

Exhibit 35

SAIN OLD TESTAMENT CURRICULUM

Quarter	Year 1	Year 2	Year 3	Year 4	Year 5	Year 6
1	Old Test. Survey	Law II (Numbers & Deuteronomy)	2 Samuel	Ezra Nehemiah	Proverbs & Song of Solomon	Ezekiel
2	Genesis	Joshua	1 Kings	Esther	Ecclesiastes	Daniel
3	Exodus	Judges Ruth	2 Kings	Job	Isaiah	Minor Prophets I (Hosea-Micah)
4	Law I (Leviticus & Numbers)	1 Samuel	1&2 Chronicles	Psalms	Jeremiah	Minor Prophets (Nahum-Malachi)

Exhibit 36

SAIN NEW TESTAMENT CURRICULUM

Quarter	Year 1	Year 2	Year 3	Year 4	Year 5	Year 6
1	New Testament Survey	Denominational Doctrines	Romans I Evidences	Christian Evidences	Church History I	James
2	Matthew	John	Romans II	Galatians	Church History II	1 Peter 2 Peter Jude
3	Mark	Acts I	1 Corinthians	Ephesians Colossians Philippians	1 Timothy 2 Timothy Titus	1 John 2 John 3 John
4	Luke	Acts II	2 Corinthians	1 Thessalonians	Hebrews 2 Thessalonians Philemon	Revelation

Exhibit 37

FOREST PARK 4ᵗʰ - 12ᵗʰ GRADE CURRICULUM

Year 1

Quarter	4-6 Grades	7-8 Grades	9-11 Grades	12 Grade
1	Life of Joseph	James, 1&2 Peter 1-3 John, Jude	Ruth, Lives of Samuel & Saul in 1 Samuel	Fleshly Sins, Marriage & Divorce
2	Life of Daniel	Life of Moses Exodus 21 thru Leviticus, Numbers, Deuteronomy	Church History	Classroom Teaching Internship
3	Jesus Early Life & First Year of His Ministry	Hebrews	Third year of Jesus' Ministry	Finances
4	Lives of Adam, Noah, and Job	Second Year of Jesus' Ministry	Revelation	Place in Church Organization & Mission

Year 2

Quarter	4-6 Grades	7-8 Grades	9-11 Grades	12 Grade
1	Life of Moses to Exodus 20	Stewardship & Evangelism	Stewardship & Evangelism	Fleshly Sins, Marriage & Divorce
2	Book of Joshua	Paul's Conversion & Missionary Journeys 1 & 2, Acts 9-18:22, 1&2Thessalonians	Problems Facing Teens	Classroom Teaching Internship

179

Quarter	4-6 Grades	7-8 Grades	9-11 Grades	12 Grade
3	Last Week of Jesus' Life	Christian Evidences	Christian Evidences	Finances
4	Crucifixion, Burial, Resurrection, & Ascension of Jesus	Book of Judges	Divided Kingdom 2 Kings, 2 Chronicles Joel, Jonah, Amos, Hosea, Isaiah, Micah Zephaniah, Nahum, Jeremiah, Lamentations Habakkuk, Daniel, Ezekiel, Obadiah	Place in Church Organization & Mission
Year 3				
1	Acts 1-8 Life of Peter Early Life of the Church	Epistles of James, 1&2 Peter, 1-3 John & Jude	Ezekiel, Ezra, Haggai, Zechariah, Esther, Nehemiah, Malachi	Fleshly Sins, Marriage & Divorce
2	Lives of Abraham, Isaac & Jacob	Life of Moses Exodus 21 thru Leviticus, Numbers &Deuteronomy	Paul's 3rd Journey Acts 18-19, 1&2 Corinthians, Galatians, Romans 1-12	Classroom Teaching Internship
3	Life of David 2 Samuel, 1 Chronicles, & Psalms	Hebrews	Paul's 3rd Journey Romans 13-16, Acts 20-28 Colossians, Ephesians. Philemon, Philippians, 1&2 Timothy& Titus	Finances
4	Life of Solomon 1Kings, 2 Chron., Proverbs, Ecclesiastes, & Song of Solomon	Second Year of Jesus' Ministry	Problems Facing Teens	Place in Church Organization & Mission

Exhibit 38

LETTER TO PARENTS YOUTH MINISTRY

Dear Parents,

As you know, we have been in the process of restructuring our youth ministry. Through the diligent efforts of our team leaders we have completed preparations for the coming year. Attached is the activities schedule that was given to your children during their Bible class last Sunday. The elders believe that the activities planned for this year represent a comprehensive program that will be of great benefit to our youth IF the children and their parents support and participate in all aspects of it.

The team leaders have been given the authority and responsibility to develop, plan and carry out each activity in their area. They will be in contact with you and your children as these events approach in order to solicit your support and involvement. If you have questions or suggestions concerning certain activities, please contact the team leader or their assistants over that area. They are as follows:

Team One (Youth Rally) –   Names
Team Two (Evangelism) -   Names
Team Three (Service Projects) -   Names
Team Four (Retreats) -   Names
Team Five (Social Activities) -   Names
Team Six (Pre-Teens) -   Names

The elders are excited about our new youth ministry. We believe it is a vital part of our many ongoing ministries that will contribute to the spiritual and numerical growth of the body of Christ at (congregation name)

The elders,

_____   _____

_____   _____

Enclosure

Exhibit 39

Youth Rally Planning Outline

Theme:
Text:
Date:
Topics:

Committees/Leaders
1. Speakers/member names
2. Advertising/member names
3. Fun activities/member names
4. Housing/member names
5. Food/member names
6. Registration/member names
7. Building setup/cleanup/member names
8. Art/Decorations/member names

Advertising/Mailing
1. Develop master mailing list with names of congregations.
2. Develop and mail brochure to obtain attendance information(date, topic, housing) by designated deadline.
3. Purchase notepads/pencils.
4. Assign callers to contact congregations.

Fun Activities
1. Plan and develop appropriate activities with specified time limits.
2. Keep receipts for all purchases of materials.

Housing
1. Announce to congregation the need for housing at least two months in advance verbally and in the bulletin.
2. Keep a log of those who have volunteered to house children.
3. When RSVP's are received notify volunteers of who and how many they will be housing.
4. Notify volunteers of the time they will need to be at the building to pick up their guests.
5. Ensure guests have transportation to the building from their guest homes.

Speakers/Worship

1. Mail topics and text to speakers – request biographical information.
2. Request that each first time speaker complete the speakers questionnaire (Exhibit 15).
3. Secure housing for out of town speakers.
4. Special speaker requests (audio/visual, copying, etc.).
5. Obtain checks for speakers before day of rally.

Building/Grounds Setup/Cleanup

1. Air conditioning
2. Sound room
3. Setup chairs
4. Open/Close building
5. Adult supervision

Exhibit 40

Medical Release Form

This is authorization and release for emergency medical treatment for my child, _____.

The intent of this authorization and release is to provide for the emergency medical treatment of my child, a minor, arising from unforeseen emergencies and to permit competent medical treatment where such authorization is required by the attending medical practitioner or medical institution prior to treatment.

Listed below are any known allergies, medicine currently being taken or other medical history which should be considered in the event emergency medical treatment is performed. (Please list over-the-counter medicine your child is currently taking.)

_____

_____

_____

Date of last tetanus shot _____

Date of birth _____/_____/_____

Medical insurance provider (copy of insurance card)

Subscriber's name _____

Phone number(s) where parents/guardian can be reached:

_____

_____

_____

I authorize the attending teachers/personnel from the (congregation name) to render, seek and authorize competent medical treatment as stated above. Furthermore, I release the above mentioned teachers/personnel and (congregation name) from any liability for any accident or injury that might be incurred.

_____   _____
Witness   Parent/Guardian

_____
Date

* Form should be approved by your attorney or legal council

Exhibit 41

PRE-TEEN PARENTS LETTER

Dear Parents,

Our children are a very important part of the family of God at (congregation).

The elders want to commend the adults who lead in providing our youth with opportunities to serve, grow spiritually and fellowship with other Christian children. As human beings, we are influenced by those with whom we come in contact. The more time our youth spend with other Christians the more likely they are to develop Christian values and habits.

With that thought in mind, we are planning a new program for our children in the first to sixth grade. One Saturday each month starting in (month) there will be an activity for them as shown on the enclosed agenda. (Name) has volunteered to head up this work.

All the planning and coordination in the world will not benefit our pre-teens if they don't take part in the opportunities we provide for them to make friends with those children from families with similar Christian values. In order to participate they must have your support and encouragement. Please build your family schedules around these events whenever possible and help (name) and the other volunteers make this effort a success.

If you have any questions please contact (name).

The Elders,

_____   _____

_____   _____

Enclosure

Exhibit 42

Lads to Leaders Information

What scholarships are available? Over $600,000 in scholarships are offered to various Christian universities for those students who meet the requirements.

How to start a Lads to Leader & Leaderettes Program at your congregation?

1. Review the Lads Website at www.lads-to-leaders.org.
2. Call or e-mail the National Service Center to schedule a meeting between your congregation's leaders and a Lads representative.
3. Schedule a Workshop and planning session by a Lads representative.
4. Hold a "kick-off" event to sign up participants.

Contact Information

5280 West Alabama Christian Drive
Montgomery, Alabama 36109

Phone: 334-215-0251
Fax: 334-215-0856

E-mail: ladsoffice@lads-to-leaders.org

Exhibit 43

POTENTIAL PREACHER EVALUATION FORM

Candidate: _____

Elder: _____

* DQ = Disqualified

Category	Points	Candidate
Age Range		
30-35	3	_____
36-45	5	
46-51	4	
52-65	2	
66+	1	
Marital Status		
Single	DQ-5	_____
Divorced	DQ-5	
Married	3-5	
Married w/c	5	
Doctrinal Positions		
Marriage/Divorce/Re	DQ-5	_____
Discipline	DQ-5	_____
Fellowship	DQ-5	_____
Music	DQ-5	_____
(Other topics)	DQ-5	_____
Personal Traits		
Personality	1-5	_____
Appearance	1-5	_____
Work ethic	1-5	_____
Study habits	1-5	_____
People skills	1-5	_____
Visiting	1-5	_____

Category	Points	Candidate
Wife		
Personality	1-5	_____
Doctrinal positions	DQ-5	_____
Appearance	1-5	_____
Teaching ability/experience	1-5	_____
Personal evangelism	1-5	_____
Children @ home		
Behavior	1-5	_____
Appearance	1-5	_____
Respect for authority	1-5	_____
Example/Involvement	1-5	_____
Sermons		
Content	1-5	_____
Delivery	1-5	_____
Structure	1-5	_____
PowerPoint/etc	1-5	_____
Variety	1-5	_____
Bible class teacher	1-5	_____
Elder/Preacher Relations		
Elder's authority	DQ-5	_____
Oversight of preacher	1-5	_____
Annual evaluation	1-5	_____
Willingness to improve in weak areas	1-5	_____
References		
Previous congregations	DQ-5	_____
Individuals	DQ-5	_____
Bible Version		
KJ/NKJ	1-5	_____
ESV	1-5	_____
ASV	1-5	_____
Others	DQ-5	_____
Foreign Evangelism		
Experience	1-5	_____
Attitude	1-5	_____
Willingness to go	1-5	_____

Category	Points	Candidate
Writing ability		
Bulletin articles	1-5	_____
Published articles	1-5	_____
Books published	1-5	_____
Public Speaking Experience		
Gospel meetings	1-5	_____
Lectureships	1-5	_____
Youth		
Experience	1-5	_____
Attitude	1-5	_____
Education		
Degrees/School	1-5	_____
Continuing education	1-5	_____
Questionnaire	DQ-5	_____
Personal Goals	1-5	_____
Hobbies Outside the church	1-5	_____
Other Topics?	1-5	_____
General Impression	1-5	_____
Would you look forward to hearing him every Sunday?	1-5	_____
TOTAL POINTS		_____
AVERAGE POINTS FOR ALL ELDERS		_____

Exhibit 44

PREACHER'S DUTIES/RESPONSIBILITIES

Duties listed below are in order of importance as determined by the elders.

1. Preaching/Teaching

    a. Bringing sound gospel sermons.

    b. Bringing sermons that are needed for edification of the congregation. The elders will, at times, request lessons on specific topics.

    c. Teaching Bible classes as requested by the Bible school director or elders.

    d. Sufficient personal study to accomplish the above.

2. Visiting members and non-members

    a. Hospital visits to members and non-members.

    b. Visits to bereaved members.

    c. Visits to shut-ins/elderly members.

    d. Visits to local visitors.

3. Bible Studies/Counseling with members and non-members

4. Special Assignments

5. Office Administration

    a. Staff supervision.

    b. Writing and editing the bulletin and other publications.

    c. Visits and meetings with elders.

What the elders owe the preacher:

1. Priorities for your position
2. Specific guidelines within each of these priority areas
3. Objective rating scheme

Numerical Rating Scheme:

1. Unacceptable
2. Needs improvement
3. Satisfactory
4. Above average
5. Exceptional

What the preacher owes the elders:

1. Satisfactory performance in each assigned area with appropriate emphasis by priority.
2. Adequate preparation for all attended meetings to include completion of a weekly activity report and oral status of other assignments.

1. Sermons/Class Teaching/Preparation

Elders' Objectives:

1. Preach three out of five sermons each month on subjects other than "first principles."
2. Plan a brief series on the "dangers of modern translations."
3. Preach requested topics within three weeks of request.
4. Devote 15-18 hours each week in preparation of sermons and classes.
5. Preach two lessons on church discipline.
6. Submit personal objectives to elders at time of annual review.

Preacher's Objectives:

1._____
2._____
3._____
4._____

Review:

_____
_____
_____
_____
_____

Elders' Objectives for (year):

_____
_____
_____
_____
_____

Preacher's Objectives for (year):

_____
_____
_____
_____
_____

Rating: Preaching _____   Teaching: _____

2. Visiting

Elders Objectives:
1. Visit shut-ins at least once each quarter.
2. Visit new members within 3 weeks of becoming members.
3. Visit hospitalized members.
4. Visit bereaved members.
5. Send letter to baptized children of members.

Preacher's Objectives:

_____

_____

_____

_____

Review:

_____

_____

_____

_____

Elders' Objectives for (year):

_____

_____

_____

_____

Preacher's Objectives for (year):

_____

_____

_____

_____

Rating: _____

3. Bible Studies/Counseling with members/non-members

Elders' Objectives:
1. Maintain at least one on-going personal Bible study every week.
2. Increase the hours per week devoted to this area to a minimum of five.

Preacher's Objectives:

_____
_____
_____
_____

Review:

_____
_____
_____
_____

Elders' Objectives for (year):

_____
_____
_____
_____

Preacher's Objectives for (year):

_____
_____
_____
_____

Rating: _____

4. Special Assignments

Elders' Objectives:

1. Plan and implement a Family Seminar.

Preacher's Objectives:

_____
_____
_____

Review:

_____
_____
_____

Elders' Objectives for (year):

_____
_____

Preacher's Objectives for (year):

_____

_____

_____

Rating: _____

5. *Office Administration*

Elder's Objectives:

1. Continue to produce personal articles for Bulletin.

Preacher's Objectives:

_____

_____

_____

Review:

_____

_____

_____

Elders' Objectives for (year):

_____

_____

_____

Preacher's Objectives for (year):

_____

_____

_____

Rating: _____   **Overall Rating:** _____

Review date: ____/____/_____

Elders:

_____   _____

_____   _____

Preacher:

_____

Exhibit 45

PREACHER'S WEEKLY ACTIVITY REPORT

Week of: _____   Total Hours: _____

Worship/Bible classes: _____ hrs   Church related mtgs: _____ hrs

Sermon prep/study: _____ hrs   General office work: _____ hrs

Radio work: _____ hrs   Bulletin articles: _____ hrs

Hospital visits: _____ hrs

      1. _____   2. _____

      3. _____   4. _____

Member visits: _____ hrs

      1. _____   2. _____

      3. _____   4. _____

Non-member visits: _____ hrs

      1. _____   2. _____

      3. _____   4. _____

Bible studies: _____ hrs

      1. _____   2. _____

      3. _____   4. _____

Elderly/Shut-in visits: _____ hrs

      1. _____   2. _____

      3. _____   4. _____

Sermon topics:

A.M. _____

P.M. _____

Exhibit 46

GOSPEL MEETING SCHEDULE

Date	Speaker	Status	Subject	Questionnaire	Phone
xx/xx/xxxx	K. Smith	Accepted	Marriage	On file	xxx-xxx-xxxx
xx/xx/xxxx	J. Dodd	Accepted	Family	On file	xxx-xxx-xxxx
xx/xx/xxxx	L. Jones	Pending	Christian Evidences	Pending	xxx-xxx-xxxx
xx/xx/xxxx	F. Wilson	Pending	TBD	Pending	xxx-xxx-xxxx

Exhibit 47

Gospel Meeting Initial Letter to Speaker

Dear Brother _____,

We are looking forward to you speaking at (your congregation) on (verbally agreed dates).

As shepherds of the flock at (your congregation) we are greatly concerned about the various doctrines that are presently plaguing and dividing the Lord's church. We feel a strong obligation to do what we can to ensure that the flock here is fed only from God's Word and not from the doctrines of men. This is one of the many responsibilities that God has given to us as shepherds.

We realize that we only have authority over and responsibility for those that teach at (your congregation) and those sent out from (your congregation) to teach others. However, this responsibility does include those we invite speak to our members.

For this reason and as a matter of expedience, we have compiled the attached questionnaire that deals with various doctrines and areas of potential division in the church today. We do not intend to imply that this document is an exhaustive discussion of all Biblical truths.

These questions are not intended to offend you or call your faith into question. This is simply an attempt to fulfill our duties to our flock and to God (1Peter 5:2; Acts 20:28-30). Your response will, of course, be kept strictly confidential.

Please complete the enclosed questionnaire and return it to us as soon as possible.

In Christian love,

The elders, (your congregation)

_____   _____

_____   _____

Encl.

Exhibit 48

Gospel Meeting Checklist

Meeting dates: _____ Speaker: _____

Address: _____

_____

Phone: _____ E-mail: _____

General topic: _____

Lesson topics: 1. _____
                2. _____
                3. _____
                4. _____
                5. _____

Questionnaire sent: _____

Questionnaire received: _____

Lodging arrangements: hotel reservations

_____

_____

Church house: _____

Member's house: _____

Airline reservations: _____

_____

Private vehicle: _____

Sunday

Breakfast: _____

Lunch: _____

Dinner: _____

- Planned activities: _____

Monday

Breakfast: _____

Lunch: _____

Dinner: _____

- Planned activities: _____

Tuesday

Breakfast: _____

Lunch: _____

Dinner: _____

- Planned activities: _____

Wednesday

Breakfast: _____

Lunch: _____

Dinner: _____

- Planned activities: _____

Thursday

Breakfast: _____

Lunch: _____

Dinner: _____

- Planned activities: _____

Exhibit 49

GOSPEL MEETING COVER LETTER

Dear Brother: _____,

We have received your response to our letter and are looking forward to your speaking at our (date) meeting on the subject of (subject).

Enclosed for your convenience is our travel expense form. Please complete the information and give it to one of the elders prior to the end of the meeting. You will be given a separate check for these expenses.

We believe it is important for both parties to be in agreement concerning the remuneration for your speaking services prior to your arrival. We are proposing a payment of ($ amount) for each of the (# of lessons) presented during this meeting for a total compensation of ($ amount). If for any reason this amount is unacceptable, please contact us immediately so that we may discuss this matter.

For the elders,

(Name of elder)

Exhibit 50

ITEMIZED TRAVEL EXPENSE RECORD
FOR VISITING SPEAKERS

Speaker: _____

Meeting dates: _____

    Mileage: _____ miles @ (GSA Rate) per mile = $ _____

    Meals: $ _____

    Airfare: $ _____

    Ground transportation: $ _____

    Parking: $ _____

    Misc. _____ $ _____

             _____ $ _____

Total: $ _____

Signature: _____

Date: _____

Exhibit 51

MEETING EVALUATION

(Comments/Observations/Recommendations)

Elders:

_____
_____
_____
_____
_____
_____

Deacons:

_____
_____
_____
_____
_____
_____

Members:

_____
_____
_____
_____
_____
_____

Exhibit 52

MINISTRY BUDGET PROPOSAL

Care Groups

Activity	Estimated Cost
Pavilion rental	$300
Van parking (baseball game)	$50
New member lunch	$50
Total	$400

Youth

Activity	Estimated Cost
Youth rally	$400
Cookout	$200
Retreat	$500
Total	$1,100

Exhibit 53

ELDERS BUDGET PRESENTATION

Introduction

Welcome

Purpose of Presentation – Present and explain our (year) budget (explain to visitors this is an annual presentation).

Review (year) budget vs. contributions: To set the stage for our review of the (year) budget I want to recap our financial status through October of this year. Our contributions have been averaging about $680 over our weekly budget through October. This puts our contributions about $25,000 over budget to date.

(year) Budget

The (year) budget, which has been reviewed and approved by our deacons, is about $350 a week higher than our (year) budget, but $325 below our (year) weekly contribution average. We have taken a conservative approach for next year. We have no outstanding loans or credit card balances. We do carry an emergency reserve for unforeseen events such as A/C or furnace replacement, and sewage problems. We will periodically review the budget throughout next year and make adjustments if necessary.

Challenge

As good stewards, we must put the Lord first with our physical blessings. That means from a practical standpoint that we should determine what level of giving is appropriate, then determine how we will live on the remaining income we have available. We should never base our giving on what is "left over" after day to day expenses have been paid. Luke tells us in Luke 6:38 that our return will be much greater than our investment.

Purpose Sheets

Next Sunday we will pass out purpose sheets for (year). Some of our newer members may not be familiar with these. They are not a contract. No one is "legally" bound by this document, but they do provide the elders an estimate of what funds we will have to work with next year. Each year we do not receive these sheets from every member. To understand how important this information is in our planning, consider how you would plan your personal spending for (year) if your employer would not tell you how much you would be making each week or even if he was going to pay you each week? What if he occasionally forgot to pay or was out of town on vacation or sick on payday and didn't get around to making out your paycheck, then the next week he didn't bother to make up for the missed paycheck? You can see the challenge we face without your Purpose Sheets.

The elders make obligations to many people and church related organizations based on our budget each year. These people depend on us to keep our word. Please help us to do that.

Agenda

Opening prayer – James

Front page – John

Back page – Bill

Q & A – Tom

Members who wish to privately discuss the budget with the elders should contact one of us to schedule a meeting for this week.

Exhibit 54

CHURCH OF CHRIST
(YEAR) BUDGET PROPOSAL
(Excel Spreadsheet)

	(year) Budget	(year) YTD 10/31/xx	(year) Budget
Local Outreach			
Direct Mail	$15,000	$14,500	$18,000
Gospel Meetings	1,400	1,500	1,700
Promotions	2,500	2,000	2,500
Total Local Outreach	**18,900**	**18,000**	**22,200**
	%_____	%_____	%_____
Foreign Missions			
Africa	8,000	7,000	9,000
Russia	4,000	4,000	5,000
Total Foreign Missions	**12,000**	**11,000**	**14,000**
	%_____	%_____	%_____
Benevolence			
Agape	5,000	4,000	5,000
Children's Home	6,000	5,000	6,000
Gen. Benevolence	8,000	4,000	8,000
Total Benevolence	**19,000**	**13,000**	**19,000**
	%_____	%_____	%_____
Local Work			
Bible School	3,000	2,800	4,000
Youth	1,500	1,300	1,700
Care Groups	1,000	1,000	1,200
Salaries	75,000	60,000	80,000
	%_____	%_____	%_____
Total Local Work	**80,500**	**65,100**	**86,900**
	%_____	%_____	%_____
Local Ops Expenses			
Building Main.	15,000	12,000	17,000
Insurance	10,000	10,000	11,000
Utilities	21,000	18,000	22,000
	%_____	%_____	%_____
Total Local Ops	**46,000**	**40,000**	**50,000**
	%_____	%_____	%_____
TOTALS	**176,400**	**147,100**	**192,100**
Required Weekly Cont.	3,392	3,065	3,694

Exhibit 55

PURPOSE SHEET

My purpose sheet for the year_____

    Realizing how much the Lord has blessed me(us) and being more aware of my(our) responsibility to Him, I(we) plan (the Lord willing) to give _____ per week or month (circle one), to the church of Christ, (address). I (we) believe this donation will be giving as I (we) have prospered as well as giving liberally (1Corinthians 16:1-2; 2Corinthians 9:7). I (we) believe that my (our) first obligation in the Lord's work is to my (our) home congregation. Should something arise which would keep me (us) from giving the above amount, I (we) will notify the eldership.

_____
(Signed)

_____
(Month)   (Day)   (Year)

* This information is for the elder's use only and will be held in strictest confidence.

Exhibit 56

MONTHLY CONTRIBUTIONS

JULY (YEAR)

Week	Mbr Contrib.	Return Ck Pd.	Return Ck& Fee	Total Contrib.
July 5th	$3,505			$3,505
July 12th	3,420			3,240
July 19th	2,900			2,900
July 26th	4,010			4,010
Total				**13,655**

Exhibit 57

MONTHLY CONTRIBUTIONS REPORT (YEAR)
YEAR-TO-DATE

Month	Contribution	Budget	Difference	Over/Under for Year
January	$15,404	$14,000	$1,404	$1,404
February	13,205	14,000	(795)	609
March	14,500	14,000	500	1,109
April	18,985	17,500	1,485	2,594

* Some months have five Sundays

Exhibit 58

CHURCH OF CHRIST BUDGET AS OF 05/31/XXXX

(Excel Spreadsheet)

	(yr) Budget as of 12/31/xx	(yr) Budget	(yr)Budget as of 5/31/xx
Local Outreach			
Direct Mail	$15,000	$18,000	$8,000
Gospel Mtgs	1,400	1,700	800
Promotions	2,500	2,500	2,000
Total Local OR	**18,900**	**22,200**	**10,800**
	%_____	%_____	%_____
Foreign Missions			
Africa	8,000	9,000	5,000
Russia	4,000	5,000	2,500
Total Foreign Missions	**12,000**	**14,000**	**7,500**
	%_____	%_____	%_____
Benevolence			
Agape	5,000	5,000	1,600
Children's Home	6,000	6,000	2,000
Gen. Benevolence	8,000	8,000	1,600
Total Benevolence	**19,000**	**19,000**	**5,200**
	%_____	%_____	%_____
Local Work			
Bible School	3,000	4,000	1,600
Youth	1,500	1,700	680
Care Groups	1,000	1,200	480
Salaries	75,000	80,000	34,760
Total Local Work	**80,500**	**86,900**	**37,520**
	%_____	%_____	%_____
Local Ops Expenses			
Building Main.	15,000	17,000	6,800
Insurance	10,000	11,000	4,400
Utilities	21,000	22,000	8,800
Total Local Ops	**46,000**	**50,000**	**20,000**
	%_____	%_____	%_____
TOTALS	**176,400**	**192,100**	**81,020**
Required Weekly Cont.	3,392	3,694	3,858

Exhibit 59

SPECIAL/ESCROW ACCOUNT REPORT

AS OF 5/31/XX

(Excel Spreadsheet)

	Beginning Balance	Deposits	Disbursements	Ending Balance
Total Cash on Hand	**$13,500**	**$3,200**	**$(3,750)**	**$12,950**
Itemized				
Gospel meetings	2,000		(250)	1,750
Youth	1,500	200		1,700
Property main.	3,000		(1,500)	1,500
Insurance	7,000	3,000	(2,000)	8,000
Reconciling Totals	**13,500**	**3,200**	**(3,750)**	**12,950**

Exhibit 60

(Year) Check Request

Name _____ $_____

Address _____

City _____ State_____ Zip _____

Purpose _____

Special instructions _____

Date ___/____/_____ Check #_____ Approval _____

CHARGE TO:

____ 001 AGAPE   ____ 006 Office equipment

____ 002 Benevolence   ____ 007 Utilities

____ 003 Bible school supplies   ____ 008 Telephone

____ 004 Direct mail   ____ 009 Utilities

____ 005 Gospel meetings   ____ 010 Youth

Exhibit 61

Elder nomination Process

Publicly read Acts 14:23; Titus 1:5; 1 Timothy 3:1-7

"Due to the size and many ministries at our congregation, we have recognized the need for additional elders for some time and have been working toward that objective. We have held training classes, attended seminars, interviewed several men and their wives in the congregation and prayed fervently to God for guidance in this grave responsibility."

"We have selected John Doe for your consideration. John, would you, Jane and your children (names) please stand."

If anyone in the congregation knows of a scriptural reason why John should not be appointed to the office of elder, we would ask that you submit a signed statement to the elders outlining your reasons by this Friday (date)."

"If we do not receive a response, we intend to install John next Sunday (date)."

Prayer

Exhibit 62

ELDER INSTALLATION PROCESS

"Last Sunday John Doe's name was placed before the congregation for your consideration as an elder. We have not received any scriptural reasons why John should not be appointed. Therefore, we will install him this morning."

"John and Jane, please stand with the elders and their wives."

Read Acts 20:17, 28-32; Hebrews 13:17; 1Peter 5:1-4; 1Corinthians 16:13,14

"This is grave and serious responsibility. John, do you understand the qualifications and accept the responsibilities of the work of elder at the (name) Church of Christ?"

"Jane, do you accept the responsibilities of an elder's wife and will you, to the best of your ability, support John as an elder?"

May God bless you both and give you a long life to carry out this great work."

Prayer

Exhibit 63

STEWARDSHIP DISCUSSION OUTLINE

1. 1. Elders discuss the seriousness of their God given responsibilities, their love for souls and fear of God (Hebrews 13:17).

2. Their responsibilities as shepherds of this flock to constantly watch for signs of straying members knowing Satan is also watching.

3. Signs such as inconsistent attendance, social habits, children, marriages, etc.

4. Review member's giving annually and identify inconsistencies that may indicate a problem and discuss with members.

5. Our responsibility: Ensure that members understand Bible teaching on stewardship and the dangers of not being faithful stewards.

6. Members responsibility: Determine scriptural level and consistency of giving based on Bible teaching.

7. Nothing leaves the room, strict confidence, sensitive subject, we understand. World and Satan can pull any of us into materialism.

Exhibit 64

PROSPECTIVE MEMBER'S PACKAGE

Cover Page

Church Name
Address
Phone
Mailing Address
E-mail Address
Website

Page Two

I. **Where we stand**

    a. Authority of Jesus Christ (Matthew 28:18)

    b. Autonomy of local congregations (Acts 20:28)

    c. Worship according to the New Testament (John 4:24)

    d. Christians are expected to live their lives in accordance with the New Testament (Titus 2:11-13)

    e. The Identity of the Lord's church (Ephesians 1:23-35)

II. **A word from the elders**

As shepherds of the flock at (name) church of Christ we are greatly concerned over the various doctrines that are presently plaguing and dividing the church of our Lord. We feel a great obligation to do what we can to ensure that this flock is fed only from God's Word and not from the doctrines of men. This is a responsibility that God has given us as shepherds.

We realize that we only have authority over and responsibility for those Christians who are members of this congregation.

For these reasons and as a matter of expediency, we have compiled the following statements that set forth what we believe the Bible to state or teach in several areas that seem to be dividing the church today. We do not intend to imply that this is an exhaustive statement of all truths.

Please read over these statements. We would appreciate your comments and always wish to please the Father and our Lord Jesus Christ.

1. The Bible was given by the inspiration of God and all parts of the Old and New Testaments were written by men inspired by God (2Timothy 3:16).

2. The Bible is complete and is sufficient to guide all men to eternal salvation (2Peter 1:3; Jude 3).

3. God created the heavens and the earth and all living things therein in six (24 hour) days (Genesis 1; Exodus 20:11).

4. God destroyed all mankind in a universal flood, except Noah and his family in the ark - all that crept on the land or flew in the air, was destroyed(Genesis 7).

5. The Bible states that there is only one church (Ephesians 4:4) whose head is Christ (Ephesians 5:23) and only those who are baptized into Christ are added to that one church by God (Acts 2:47).

6. The Bible teaches that the Kingdom of God on earth and the church are the same (Matthew 16:18-19) and that the church was established on the day of Pentecost (Acts 2).

7. The Bible states that all spiritual blessings are in Christ (Ephesians 1:3). If we turn from Christ after we have known and obeyed Him, and do not repent, the spiritual blessings (eternal life) will be taken away (2Peter 2:21).

8. The Bible states that sin is a transgression of the law (1John 3:4) and that all have sinned (Romans 3:23). When we reach the age that we are accountable for these sins, we must be baptized (by burial in water) into Christ in order to receive remission of these sins (Acts 2:38; Mark 16:16).

9. The New Testament specifies only one kind of music to be used in worship to God and that is singing (Colossians 3:16; Ephesians 5:19). Anything else, such as playing musical instruments, humming or imitating musical instruments with our mouth, is not commanded and is not pleasing to God in our worship to Him. There is also no example of choirs, solos or singing groups in worship to God since these verses state we are to speak to one another in psalms, hymns and spiritual songs.

10. The Bible teaches that the Lord's Supper should be taken only on the first day of the week as part of our worship to God and every week has a first day (1Corinthians 11:20; Acts 20:7).

11. The Bible states that a woman may not lead a prayer, teach, or be in a position of authority over a Christian man (1Timothy 2:11,12; 1Corinthians 14:34).

12. The Bible teaches that the Holy Spirit, which enabled first century Christians to perform miracles to confirm the Word, no longer works in this manner, since we now have the complete will of God (Acts 8:18; 1Corinthians 13:8-10).

13. The Bible states that the church is to withdraw fellowship from those in the church who walk disorderly in order to restore them and to purge sin from the church (2Thessalonians 3:6,14; 1Timothy 6:3-5; 1Corinthians 5:7, 9-13).

14. The Bible teaches that false teachers are to be marked and avoided. (Romans 16:17; Jude 9-11; Titus 1:9-11; 2Timothy 4:3). This would include any activity, meeting or lectureship that is organized and sponsored by known false teachers and where false teaching is promoted. If we fellowship false teachers we share in their evil deeds (2John 9-11). We, the elders, do not believe one is avoiding false teachers if he continually attends such events.

15. The Bible states that marriage is for life and the only reason for divorce in God's eyes is fornication; then the only one free to remarry is the innocent party (Matthew 5:32; 19:9; Luke 16:18).

16. The Bible teaches we should help one another overcome our weaknesses, but does not command that we confess our every sin (of our hearts) to another human being in order to be forgiven of that sin. (James 5:16; 1John 1:9).

These truths are stated in God's Word and we believe that we must follow God's Word in order to be pleasing to Him. (1Peter 2:5).

III. Our elders

John Doe (phone)
        Care groups
        Involvement
        Local outreach
        Preaching
        Delinquents

Jim Stone (phone)
        Office
        Missions
        Finances
        Building/Grounds

Howard Smith (phone)
        Benevolence
        Youth
        Transportation

Bob Wheeler (phone)
        Bible school
        Gospel meetings

IV. Our deacons

Name	Phone	Ministry
John Williams	XXX–XXX-XXXX	Youth
Ted Smith	XXX-XXX-XXXX	Bible School

V. Our preacher

Bob Wright (phone)

VI. Ministries

Bible school	Missions
Benevolence	Youth
Local outreach	Care groups

Exhibit 65

Prospective Member Interview Checklist

Location: _____

Attendees (all elders if possible; minimum of two):

_____   _____

_____   _____

Time: _____

Topics:

1. Introduction by current chairman or designee (explain purpose of meeting).

2. Each elder give a short bio of his background, family, duties, etc. Chairman of meeting speak for those elders not in attendance.

3. Provide opportunity for person(s) to give information about themselves, family, work, previous congregation (left in good standing?), hobbies, interests.

4. Ask if they have any questions for the elders.

5. Ask if they have been married before and if so, what the circumstances of their divorce, if applicable, were.

6. Ask if they are familiar with the doctrine of church discipline. If not, explain and stress this practice here.

7. Stress the expectation of the elders that all members be involved in serving in some capacity here. Explain involvement process.

8. Emphasize the expectation that they be faithful in attendance on Sundays, Wednesdays, Gospel meetings.

9. Ask if they have any spiritual needs.

10. Close with prayer.

Exhibit 66

New Member Information Request

Baptized _____   Placed membership _____   Date _____

Name _____

Address _____

_____

Home phone _____   Cell phone _____

E-mail _____

His birthday _____   Christian: yes / no

Her birthday _____   Christian: yes / no

Children's names/Christian?   Birthday

_____   _____

_____   _____

_____   _____

_____   _____

Optional Information

His occupation _____   His employer _____

His work phone _____

Her occupation _____   Her employer _____

Her work phone _____

Print work information in directory? Yes/No

_____

For Office Use Only: Assigned to Care Group #_____

Exhibit 67

PLANNING MEETING COVER LETTER

Date

Dear Brothers and Sisters,

As we enter the fall of (year) time is rapidly approaching when the elders will be making plans for our activities in (year). This year we have experienced wonderful spiritual and numerical growth and we want those trends to continue next year. We believe that it is vitally important that every baptized member have an opportunity to present their ideas for continued growth to the elders. With that in mind, we have developed the attached planning form covering the major areas of work here.

We are inviting members of Life groups 1 & 2 to meet with us at 4:30 on (date) in the fellowship hall to discuss your ideas. Life groups 3 & 4 will meet with us on (date) at the same time and place. If you cannot attend your scheduled session feel free to attend the other Sunday. Babysitting and child care will be provided. Please complete the enclosed planning form prior to the meeting and be prepared to present your ideas on the various topics listed. At the end of the meetings the forms will be collected by the elders. Signatures are not necessary. We strongly encourage everyone to attend if possible. If you cannot attend, please complete the Form and give it to one of the elders as soon as possible.

We know there is a wealth of talent and ideas among our members and we look forward to hearing and reading them. Every effort will be made to incorporate as many ideas as possible into our plans for the new year.

In Christian love,

The elders

_____   _____

_____   _____

Exhibit 68

Planning Form (Year)
Church name

1. Here is what I would like to see us do in soul-winning in the new year:

2. Here is what I would like to see us do in benevolence, helping the needy:

3. Here is what I would like to see us do in our Bible classes/education:

4. Here is what I would like to see us do in local/foreign mission work:

5. Here is what I would like to see us do to strengthen homes and marriages:

6. Here is what I would like to see in special training classes:

7. Here is what I would like to see us do in helping our young people:

8. Here is what I would like to see us do to help us grow closer as a congregation:

9. Here is what I would like to see us do to improve our building/ grounds:

10. Here is what I need for my own spiritual enrichment and service:

11. Here are topics I would like to hear in sermons or Gospel meetings:

12. Other:

Exhibit 69

SAMPLE POLICIES

Weddings

Scheduling

a. Weddings/rehearsals or other uses by our members and their families. They must be scheduled through the church office at least thirty days prior to the event. The deposit is due one week after scheduling the event. Make the check payable to

_____.

b. Deposits: Specify the areas you wish to use.

   1. Auditorium only - $100
   2. Fellowship hall only - $100
   3. Auditorium and Fellowship hall - $200

Cleaning Fees

There is a cleaning fee of $200, payable to the person who is to clean before and after the wedding. This payment must be received by the church office at least one week prior to the event. Make the check payable to _____.

Decorations

a. For events held on Saturday, you may decorate after noon on the previous Thursday.

b. For events held on weekdays, you may decorate after noon the preceding day. To decorate on Wednesdays, you may do so after Bible class that evening.

c. All decorations must be removed immediately following the event.

d. Care must be taken when decorating the building. This applies to any and all areas used by the wedding party. No food or drink outside the Fellowship Hall. No drip candles or glitter may be used. It is understood that the cost of repairs for any damage to the building will be the responsibility of the wedding party. The deposit will be required up front. If there are no damages and all rules followed your deposit will be refunded one week after the wedding.

Special Notes

a. We do not allow musical instruments to be used in the building. CD music is allowed, but you must make arrangements for one of our sound technicians to play the tape or CD through the church secretary. The sound technician will disconnect the microphones in order to move the furniture. Also, there will be a $100 charge for the sound technician's services. Make the check payable to "Cash".

b. No alcoholic beverages are allowed on church property, including the building, parking lot, or any other area.

c. No smoking is on allowed on church property.

d. You may use the kitchen facilities along with the fellowship hall, but the church does not supply utensils.

e. The elders request you use one of our ministers to conduct the wedding.

f. The elders require that all functions on Saturday evening end and everyone is out of the building by 7:00 pm or the deposit will not be returned.

g. Please mail all checks to:_____

Signature: _____ Date: _____

What times will you need the heat/air on in the building?

_____

_____

AGREEMENT FORM

USE OF THE CHURCH BUILDING FOR SPECIAL EVENTS

_____   _____
Signature of the groom   Date

_____   _____
Signature of the bride   Date

Date of wedding rehearsal _____

Date of wedding/event   _____

Name of minister _____

Minister's address _____

                          _____

NOTE: Please sign and return this form to:

Funerals

The elders at (your congregation) wish to express their condolences to you and your family at this difficult time. We offer to you our comfort and our prayers to God on your behalf.

As elders of this congregation, God has placed upon us the responsibility of watching over the members of this church. This responsibility includes all activities that are carried on at our facilities. Our policies are based upon respect for the Word of God. In all things we seek to glorify Him (1Corinthians 10:31; Colossians 3:17).

The following guidelines are to be used in the planning and conduct of all funerals taking place our building and its facilities:

1. Regularly scheduled worship services and Bible classes will be given priority over the time of a funeral. Therefore the time of the funeral service must not conflict with regularly scheduled services.

2. Previously scheduled events at the church building or facilities will be given priority over a funeral time. Therefore, the time of a funeral service must not conflict with any previously scheduled event at the church building or facilities. (In the event of unusual or tragic circumstances this part of the policy may be waived by the elders).

3. The funeral service should be scheduled so as to give the church custodians time to clean and check the building before the next worship service.

4. All preachers, speakers, song leaders, prayer leaders and other positions of leadership used in the funeral service must be men who have been approved by the elders of _____. Last minute or spontaneous speakers will not be allowed unless approved by the eldership.

5. No mechanical instruments of music may be utilized in any service at the church building or the facilities.

6. Recordings of mechanical instruments of music may be used as long as the song(s) is not religious in nature nor does it make religious remarks. Songs must be approved by the elders.

7. Religious songs must be sung congregationally. Solos and singing groups may be used for non-religious songs.

8. The _____ offers its building and facilities free of charge for all funerals.

May God bless you and your family at this sad and difficult time. If you have questions or wish to discuss this policy with the elders, please call the church office at the number above and an appointment will be made.

FUNERAL FORM

Deceased: _____ Date of funeral: _____

Person/family requesting funeral: _____

Address: _____

_____

Phone: _____ Cell Phone: _____

E-mail: _____

Persons involved in funeral service:

Minister(s): _____

_____

Song leader(s): _____

_____

Prayer leader(s): _____

_____

Other speaker(s) or leaders in the service

_____

_____

_____

Comments: _____

_____

Wedding Showers

Each single member at (church name) entering into a scriptural marriage will have the option of a wedding shower hosted by their Care group. If both parties being married are members at (church name) a combined shower will be provided. If a scheduling issue exists, it is permissible for a wedding shower to be held after the wedding.

Eligibility:

a. Current members at (church name).

b. College students who are still under this elders' oversight, but who do not attend our worship services regularly during the school year due to the location of their school.

c. Missionaries and their family members living at home overseen by this eldership.

d. Anyone under the oversight of this eldership temporarily displaced due to unusual circumstances such as temporary job assignment, and military duty.

Wedding showers for individuals not meeting the eligibility criteria above must be hosted privately with individual invitations sent out. The event will not be mentioned in the bulletin. The fellowship hall may be used as for any other function, but must be scheduled through the church office to ensure there are no conflicts.

Baby Showers

a. Each married woman who is a member at (church name) will have a baby shower given by her care group for her first baby. If the fellowship hall is used it must be scheduled through the church office so there are not conflicts with dates.

b. Each married woman who is baptized or places membership and already has children will be given a baby shower by her care group for her first baby born after coming here. If the fellowship hall is used it must be scheduled through the church office so there are no conflicts with dates.

c. Any subsequent showers must be hosted privately with invitations sent out. It will be mentioned one time in the announcements. The fellowship hall may be used as for any other function and must be scheduled through the church office so there are no conflicts with dates.

Flowers

Sickness: Members who spend a minimum of one night in the hospital

Births: Members only

Deaths: Member, spouse of member, children of member, spouse of children, mother/father of member or spouse

Tables/chairs

Members desiring to borrow tables and/or chairs should contact the office prior to taking these items so that the secretary can log in the required information. Upon return of the items notify the office so they can close out the record.

Vans/buses

Church vans may be reserved only for church related functions. Contact (name) at least one week in advance providing him with the date, pickup time, length of use and purpose of the activity requiring a van(s). You must be on our insurance list of qualified drivers, complete the mileage log and ensure the inside of the vans are cleaned out after completion of your outing. Food should not be consumed in the vans during use.

Office Equipment

Church related production requests should be submitted to the office for scheduling in advance of the required date. Personnel approved to use the appropriate equipment will be given your request to complete.

Church Houses

Our houses are to be used only for church related activities such as housing missionaries or guest speakers.

Conducting business on church property

The elders ask that our members, adults or children, do not approach other members or visitors asking them to purchase such items as candy, cards, wrapping paper, etc. either in the building or parking lots. Delivery of such items, solicited elsewhere, may be done on the property if it does not disrupt the primary purposes of worship, teaching and fellowship.

Exhibit 70

LOCAL OUTREACH PROGRAM

Elder
Responsible for
Local Evangelism

Local Outreach Coordinator

Visitor/Worship	Visitor/Follow up	Community Involvement	Promotion	Bible Study
Team Leader	Team Leader	Team Leader	Team Leader	Team Leader
Team Members	Team Members	Team Members	Team Members	Team Members

Exhibit 71

LIFE GROUPS PROGRAM

Elder
Responsible for
Involvement

Life Groups Coordinator

Group 1 Leaders Assistant Leaders	Group 2 Leaders Assistant Leaders	Group 3 Leaders Assistant Leaders	Group 4 Leaders Assistant Leaders
Activity Chairpersons	Activity Chairpersons	Activity Chairpersons	Activity Chairpersons
Meals Chairpersons	Meals Chairpersons	Meals Chairperson	Meals Chairpersons
Set-up Chairperson	Set-up Chairperson	Set-up Chairperson	Set-up Chairperson
Showers Chairpersons	Showers Chairpersons	Showers Chairpersons	Showers Chairpersons
Tele/E-mail Chairpersons	Tele/E-mail Chairpersons	Tele/E-mail Chairpersons	Tele/E-mail Chairpersons
Trans. Chairperson	Trans. Chairperson	Trans. Chairperson	Trans. Chairperson
Welcome Chairperson	Welcome Chairperson	Welcome Chairperson	Welcome Chairperson
Other	Other	Other	Other

Exhibit 72

FELLOWSHIP PROGRAM

Elder
Responsible for Involvement

Fellowship Program Coordinator

Team 1	Team 2	Team 3	Team 4
Team 1 Leaders	Team 2 Leaders	Team 3 Leaders	Team 4 Leaders
Team Members	Team Members	Team Members	Team Members

Exhibit 73

YOUTH PROGRAM

Elder
Responsible for Youth

Youth Director/Minister

Youth Rally	Evangelism	Service	Retreat	Activities	Pre-Teens
Team Leader Co-Leader	Team Leader Co-Leader	Team Leader Co-Leader	Team Leader Co-Leader	Team Leader Co-Leader	Team Leader Co-Leader
Team members	Team members	Team members	Team members	Team members	Team members